1967

This book may be kept

PEPITA JIMENEZ

JUAN VALERA

INTRODUCTION AND TRANSLATION
BY HARRIET DE ONÍS

BARRON'S EDUCATIONAL SERIES, INC.
GREAT NECK, NEW YORK

JUAN VALERA

Juan Valera was one of the group of Spanish novelists often referred to as "the generation of 1868," which includes those writers who raised the novel in Spain to new eminence in the nineteenth century—Pedro Antonio de Alarcón, José María Pereda, Benito Pérez Galdós—after its decline during the decadence that nation suffered from the close of the seventeenth century until the early nineteenth.

He was born in the province of Córdoba in Andalusia on October 18, 1824, of an old and aristocratic family of liberal tradition which had contributed distinguished statesmen and soldiers to the country. He grew up during a difficult moment of Spain's history. The country had emerged from its heroic War of Independence againt Napoleon Bonaparte hopeful that the restoration of the legitimate heir, Ferdinand VII, would foster a climate of ideas and ideals that would bring it into step with the progressive spirit that was beginning to shape the destinies of the more enlightened nations of Europe. This was the attitude of the liberals; but the forces of reaction were strong, and Ferdinand tended to support them. On his death in 1833, Spain was torn by a series of fierce civil wars. His daughter, Isabel, who succeeded him, was dethroned in 1868 by a widely supported revolution, "La Gloriosa"; a new king, Amadeo of Savoy, was brought to the throne, but renounced it in less than a year; a republic was declared, which also proved of short duration, until finally, with the restoration of Isabel's son, Alfonso XII, a constitutional monarchy was set up, and peace was established which lasted with brief interruptions until the outbreak of the Civil War in 1936.

The peace of the Restoration, which brought a certain progress and prosperity to Spain, rested on the basis of a mutual tolerance between the liberal and conservative forces. In many Spaniards of the day this tolerance fostered a spirit of urbane skepticism, a distrust of the violent passions that had characterized the earlier years of the century, a tendency to avoid irreconcilable commitments, all of which Valera typified in his life and his work. As the great writer and critic Azorín says of him: "It is not easy to discover what Valera's inner feelings were. In a sense, less deeply, less transcendently, he poses the same problem as Montaigne. And Valera himself was aware of this. In 1864 he wrote: 'I confess that I am not dogmatic, and am more inclined to say with Montaigne: "What do I know?" rather than: "What is it I do not know?", as do other philosophers . . .' With his serenity and his irony—especially his irony—Valera manages to rise above personalities and issues. . . . He was a humanist of vast culture, exquisite taste, a great lover of life, a spirit of the eighteenth century, with a large dose of skepticism, tolerant, not in the least aggressive, and who knew how to dissemble in order to avoid wounding the sensibilities of others."

Valera studied law, first in Granada and then Madrid, but he soon abandoned the idea of a legal career for that of diplomacy. As he put it: "Work not being my strong point, I laid aside my lawyer's robes, and taking advantage of a favorable opportunity that presented itself, plunged headlong into diplomacy where the only requirements are the ability to dance the polka well and a taste for *foie gras*." In 1847 he was appointed attaché to the Spanish embassy in Naples, and he spent the better part of his long life, with brief intervals in Spain, in the diplomatic service of his country in a number of foreign capitals—Naples,

Lisbon, Rio de Janeiro, St. Petersburg, Washington, Paris, Vienna. But this was only one aspect of his life; the other was devoted to literature. Through study and travel he had acquired a wide culture. He spoke a number of languages, had a solid knowledge of the classics, and his clear, organized mind enabled him to absorb the best of the literature and philosophy of his day and to reflect his opinions to his countrymen in a long series of essays and articles. After Menéndez Pelayo, he was the best Spanish critic of his century.

He had exercised his talents in poetry and criticism before turning to the novel. His first novel, *Pepita Jiménez*, did not appear until 1874, when he was already fifty years old.

Spain may be said to have a vocation for the novel. Great literatures are complete organisms; they include all the genres. But there are certain forms which stand out above the others, indicating a collective vocation, and that of Spain is for the drama and the novel. This latter assertion could be substantiated by putting forward a single name, that of Cervantes, universally considered the father of the modern novel. But the appearance of a genius is not always a decisive argument, inasmuch as genius is the exception, and, like the wind, "bloweth whither it listeth." The proof of Spain's vocation is more modestly, but more firmly, grounded. It rests upon three things: the early emergence there of this literary genre; the originality and multiplicity of the forms it created; and the persistence of the vocation for this form. Valera and his generation, and the others who followed them in rapid succession—Emilia Pardo Bazán, Leopoldo Alas, Armando Palacio Valdés, Vicente Blasco Ibáñez, Ramón del Valle-Inclán, Pío Baroja—restored the novel in Spain to the high position its history had accorded it.

In the half dozen novels which represent Valera's achievement in this field, of which *Pepita Jiménez* is the most famous, and, from many points of view, the best, two things are always

present: the autobiographical element, exterior and interior, and
the background of Córdoba against which they are set, which
is, in a sense, autobiographical, too. To quote Azorín once
more: "We can define Valera as a European who received his
formation in a Spanish village; more specifically, in a certain
Andalusian village; and even more precisely, in a village of
the province of Córdoba. Not all the regions of Andalusia have
the same character. Valera never lost contact with the reality
of the village in which he was born. He travelled widely in
Europe and America; he represented Spain in various coun-
tries of Europe and America; he knew four or six living languages, and three or four dead ones. He developed an unerring
and delicate taste. And always, beneath the European exterior, we sense the presence of his native village, the nuance
of his native Andalusia." Valera's novelistic gift flows in a
narrow channel. This may well be due to the lyrical quality of
his work, to his conception of poetry as the highest form of art,
which makes it impossible for him to create beings alien to himself. It is a waste of time to seek in Valera what Leopoldo Alas
calls "the artistic altruism" of Pérez Galdós, which enabled that
master of the novel to create beings who in no wise recall or
reflect the personality of their creator. Pérez de Ayala, himself
a gifted novelist and critic, who resembled Valera in his
literary and intellectual inclinations, has analyzed with great
acumen the difference between the work of Valera and Galdós,
regarding the former as a humanist interested only in the
general and the universal, in contrast to the "humane" approach of Galdós, interested only in the individual as such.
"The humanist," says Pérez de Ayala, "sees in each person
only the generic, and therefore reveals to us the saint, the sage,
the artist, and the hero as beings of flesh and blood, with the
same inner workings as the common, the average man. But
the humane writer puts us in cordial contact with the in-

dividual quality, and digs deep into the common, the average man until he brings to light the chip, the seed of saintliness in the most sinful, of wisdom in the most foolish, of sensibility in the most doltish, of courage in the most pusillanimous."

The plot of *Pepita Jiménez* could hardly be simpler. A young man, on the point of being ordained a priest, who believes he has the firmest of vocations, goes to spend a few months with his father in a small town in Andalusia before taking his final vows. There he meets a beautiful young widow, Pepita Jiménez, and without quite knowing what is happening, falls in love with her and she with him. The rest of the book deals with the conflict in his mind and soul between his love and what he believes to be his religious vocation. In the end he realizes that what he had taken to be a call to a religious and ascetic life was only youthful pride and self-delusion. Interspersed with the love story, Valera has posed subtle problems of conscience and theology, which are never out of place, but relevant to the subject matter, and all narrated in a terse, elegant, and often ironic style. Valera was strongly averse to the social novel, the naturalistic novel, the novel as "slice of life." But neither was he a novelist of fantasy or dreams. Basically, he was a realist, but his realism was interior rather than exterior; a realism of the affections and the soul. His narrative prose seems simple because of the order he employs; it conceals from the reader the effort and skill involved, achieving that studied naturalness which comes from a writer's mastery of his métier.

In the preface to the first English translation of *Pepita Jiménez*, published in New York in 1886, Valera wrote: "My novel, both in essence and form, is distinctively national and classic. Its merit—supposing it to have such—consists in the language and style, and not in the incidents, which are of the most commonplace . . . I am an advocate of art for art's sake.

The object of art is the creation of the beautiful, and whoever applies it to any other end, of however great utility this end may be, debases it. But it may chance, through a conjunction of favorable circumstances . . . that an author's soul may become like a clear and magic mirror wherein are reflected all the ideas and all the sentiments that animate the eclectic spirit of his country . . . Herein is the explanation of the interest of *Pepita Jiménez*. It was written when Spain was agitated to its center, and everything was thrown out of its regular course by a radical revolution that . . . shook to their foundations the throne and religious unity . . . It was written when the strife raged fiercest between ancient and modern ideals . . . If I had endeavored by dialectics and by reasoning to conciliate opinions and beliefs, the disapprobation would have been general; but as the conciliating and syncretic spirit manifested itself naturally in a diverting story, everyone accepted and approved it, each one drawing from my book the conclusions that best suited himself . . . What is certain is that if it be allowable to draw any conclusion from a story, the inference that may be deduced from mine is that faith in an all-seeing and personal God, and in the love of this God, who is in the depths of the soul, even when we refuse to follow the higher vocation to which He would persuade and solicit us— even were we carried away by the violence of mundane passions to commit, like Don Luis, almost all the capital sins in a single day—elevates the soul, purifies the other emotions, sustains human dignity, and lends poetry, nobility, and holiness to the commonest state, condition, and manner of life."

After his retirement in 1895, Valera lived out the remaining years of his life in Madrid, admired and respected by all. He had suffered many sorrows, among them the death of his son; he had lost his eyesight; his bodily strength declined, but not that of his spirit. "The only thing that is still as good as during my best days is my head," he wrote. "Even outwardly it has withstood the ravages of time, for I have as much hair as when I was thirty, save that now it is snow white. My good humor and optimism have not forsaken me." He died, so to speak, with his pen in his hand. He had just finished dictating an address to be read on the occasion of the three hundredth anniversary of the publication of *Don Quixote,* and was listening as it was read back to him, when he suffered a stroke of apoplexy, dying on April 18, 1905.

For all his skepticism, his elegant detachment from the arrogant self-assurance of the left and the right, Valera always subscribed to a generous humanitarianism, putting his faith in human kindness, which may suffer doubts, but always with the firm decision not to fall into the error of the weak and the impatient, who selfishly seek the fallacious security every type of uncompromising dogmatism offers. He was a gentleman, a scholar, a writer of unique gifts, and a human being of rare quality.

Rio Piedras, Puerto Rico   HARRIET DE ONÍS
September 1963.

PEPITA JIMÉNEZ

NESCIT LABI VIRTUS[1]

The Dean of the Cathedral of ———, who died several years ago, left among his effects a bundle of loose papers tied together, which by some quirk of fortune, after passing through many hands, came into mine without the loss of a single one of the documents that comprised it. The caption on the top page of the bundle is the Latin sentence which I use as a heading above, rather than the woman's name I now give it as a title. Perhaps this caption may have contributed to the conservation of the papers, for, in the belief that it was a sermon or some theological disquisition, no one before me had even bothered to untie the red ribbon that bound them, let alone read a single page of the contents.

The bundle contains three packets of papers. The first is entitled: *Letters from my nephew*; the second, *First and Second Chronicles*; and the third *Epilogue: Letters from my brother*.

It is all in the same handwriting, which may be inferred to be the Dean's. As the whole shapes up into something like a novel, albeit with little or no plot, I at first imagined that the Dean might have wished to exercise his ingenuity on its composition in leisure hours. But, upon examining the material at greater length, and noting the natural simplicity of the style, I am now inclined to believe that there is no such novel, but rather that the letters are copies of actual correspondence,

---

[1] *Virtue cannot fall.*

which the Dean tore up, burned, or returned to their writers; and that the narrative portion, designated by the Biblical title of First and Second Chronicles, is the Dean's only contribution, intended to round out the picture with incidents not recounted in the letters.

Be that as it may, I confess that the reading of these papers has not wearied me, but, on the contrary, has rather interested me; and as everything finds its way into print nowadays, I have decided to publish them, too, without further investigation, changing only the names, so that if their bearers are living, they may not find themselves in a novel without their wish or consent.

The letters contained in the first portion seem to have been written by a very young man, with some theoretical knowledge of the world, but little experience of its ways, educated in the seminary under the wing of the Dean, his uncle. The writer seemed to possess great zeal and religious fervor and a definite vocation for the priesthood.

We shall call this youth Don Luis de Vargas.

The aforementioned manuscript, printed exactly as it was written, is as follows:

I

LETTERS FROM MY NEPHEW

Dear Uncle and revered teacher:

It is now four days since, after a pleasant trip, I arrived in this birthplace of mine where I found my father, the Vicar, and my friends and relatives all in good health. The pleasure of seeing and talking with them after so many years of absence has so absorbed me and occupied my time that I have been unable to write you until now.

Please forgive me.

As I left here such a small boy, and have come back a grown man, the impression made upon me by all those things I had retained in my memory is an odd one. Everything looks smaller to me, much smaller, but also more beautiful than my recollection of it. My father's house, immense in imagination, is, to be sure, the big house of a wealthy farmer, but smaller than the Seminary. What I now understand and appreciate more is the countryside around here. The gardens are especially delightful. What beautiful paths traverse them! Along one side, perhaps along both, the crystal-clear water flows with a pleasant purling sound. The banks of the irrigation ditches are covered with fragrant herbs and a thousand kinds of flowers. In an instant you can gather a huge bouquet of violets. Immense, majestic walnut, fig, and other trees shade the paths, and blackberry bushes, rambler roses, pomegranate trees, and honeysuckle form hedges beside them.

The multitude of little birds that gladden these fields and groves is prodigious.

I am enchanted with the gardens, and every afternoon I spend a couple of hours walking about them.

My father wants to take me to see his olive groves, his vineyards, his farms, but I have seen none of them as yet. I have not left the village and the pleasant gardens encircling it.

To be sure, the many visitors give me no rest.

No fewer than five women have come to see me, all of whom were nurses of mine, and they've all embraced and kissed me.

They call me Luisito or Don Pedro's boy, even though I am past twenty-two. They all ask my father about "the boy" when I'm not around.

I doubt that I shall have a chance to open the books I brought to read, for they don't leave me alone for a moment.

The position of political leader, which I thought a joking matter, is a very serious thing. My father is the political leader of the village.

Almost no one here can begin to understand what they call my "mania" to become a priest. These good people tell me with rustic candor that I should lay aside my ecclesiastical garb because the priesthood is all very well for the poor, but that with my prospects what I should do is marry and comfort my father's old age with half a dozen handsome, robust grandchildren.

To flatter me and my father, men and women alike say that I'm a fine-looking chap, very witty, very charming, that my eyes are mischievous and all such nonsense which distresses, displeases, and embarrasses me, even though I'm not shy and well enough acquainted with the miseries and follies of this life not to be scandalized or intimidated by anything.

The one fault they find in me is that I am very thin from study. In order to put some weight on me, they propose not to let me study nor read a line while I am here, and also to regale me with all the culinary masterpieces the village can produce. It is obvious: they are determined to fatten me. There is no family of our acquaintance that has not sent me some treat. One time it's a cake, now a *cuajado*,[2] a pyramid of pine-nut paste, or a jar of preserves.

Not only do they heap these gifts on me, sending them to the house, but in addition three or four of the most distinguished people in the village have invited me to dinner.

Tomorrow I am dining in the house of the famous Pepita Jiménez, whom you must have heard mentioned. No one here is unaware that my father is courting her.

Despite his fifty-five years, Father is so vigorous that the most gallant of the young bloods might envy him. Moreover, he has the powerful attraction of his past conquests, his fame as a former Don Juan Tenorio, and this, to some women, proves irresistible.

I have not met Pepita Jiménez as yet. Everyone says she is very beautiful. I suspect hers must be a rustic village beauty. From all that's said about her, I'm unable to determine whether she is of noble or base character; but I can say that she has great charm and allure. Pepita must be twenty years old; she is a widow; she was married only three years. She is the daughter of Doña Francisca Gálvez, the widow, as you know, of a retired captain

> Who bequeathed her at his death
> the sole legacy of his honored sword,

---

[2] *A dish made of meat, herbs, or fruits with eggs and sugar.*

as the poet says. Until she was sixteen, Pepita lived with her
mother in the most straitened circumstances, almost in penury.

She had an uncle named Don Gumersindo, who had inherited a paltry entailed estate, one of those established in by-
gone days out of ridiculous vanity. Any normal being would
have lived in constant want on the income from this property,
probably debt-ridden and debarred from the style and decorum
befitting his class; but Don Gumersindo was no ordinary
being; he was a financial genius. He couldn't be said to have
created wealth, but he had an extraordinary faculty for ab-
sorbing that of others; and as for consuming it, hardly anyone
on earth could be found upon whose maintenance, preserva-
tion, and well-being mother nature and human industry had
had to expend less effort. How he lived no one knows; but the
fact is that he did live to the age of eighty, saving his entire
income and increasing his capital by the most fully guaranteed
loans. No one here criticizes him as a usurer; rather they regard him as charitable, for, moderate in everything, he was so
even in his rate of interest. He used to charge only ten per
cent a year, whereas throughout the entire province they charge
twenty, and even thirty per cent, and still consider it low.

With such care, such industry and with his mind fixed
upon increasing and not diminishing his worldly goods, Don
Gumersindo had forgone the luxury of marrying or having
children, or even of smoking. He reached the age I mentioned
in possession of what would undoubtedly be a tidy fortune
anywhere, and, given the poverty of these villagers and the
natural exaggeration of the Andalusians, here it was accounted
enormous.

Always very neat and careful of his person, Don Gumersindo was not an unattractive old man.

The garments that made up his simple wardrobe were
somewhat threadbare, but spotless and surpassingly clean,

though from time immemorial he had worn the same cape, the same jacket, and the same trousers and waistcoat. People sometimes questioned one another in vain as to whether anyone had ever seen him appear in a new garment.

In spite of all these defects which here and elsewhere many count as virtues, albeit somewhat exaggerated, Don Gumersindo possessed excellent qualities. He was affable, helpful, sympathetic, and went out of his way to please and to make himself useful to everyone as long as it did not involve the outlay of a penny, though it might entail effort, wakeful nights, and fatigue. Merry of nature and fond of jests and jokes, he was to be found at all gatherings and festivals where he would not be expected to pay his share. Indeed, he enlivened them with his gallantry and his agreeable though not too witty conversation. He had never shown an amorous inclination toward any particular woman, but he liked them all innocently and without malice, and was the greatest old man for ten leagues around at paying the girls compliments and making them laugh.

I have already said he was Pepita's uncle. When he was approaching eighty, she was nearing sixteen. He was in good circumstances and she was destitute.

Her mother was an ordinary woman, with few endowments and coarse instincts. She adored her daughter, but she was constantly and bitterly bemoaning the privations she was suffering and the disconsolate old age and dismal death that awaited her in such poverty. Moreover, she had a son older than Pepita who had been a village libertine, a gambler, and a fighter, and who had caused her great suffering. Finally she had managed to obtain a miserable post for him in Havana, thus getting him off her hands and putting an ocean between them. Nevertheless, after a few years in Havana, the lad was discharged for bad conduct and besieged his mother with letters begging for money. With barely enough for herself and Pepita, the mother was in despair. She raged, she cursed herself and her fate with a lack of Christian resignation, and placed all her hopes on a good match for her daughter that would free her from her anxieties.

In this worrisome time, Don Gumersindo began to frequent the house of Pepita and her mother and to court Pepita with more ardor and persistence than he had hitherto shown toward others. After all, it was so far-fetched and so unlikely that a man who had passed the age of eighty without any inclination to marry should think of such madness with one foot already in the grave, that the mother, and much less Pepita, never suspected the bold intentions of Don Gumersindo. Consequently, they were both astonished and dumfounded when, one day, after various endearing remarks, halfjoking, half-serious, Don Gumersindo suddenly, without a word of warning, and with the greatest formality, asked the following categorical question:

"Will you marry me, girl?"

Though the question came after a good deal of chaffing, and thus might have been taken as a joke, and though she was inexperienced in worldly matters, Pepita knew, by a sort of sixth sense that women, and, above all, girls, no matter how naive, possess, that it was intended seriously. She turned cherry-red and made no reply. The mother answered for her.

"Don't be ill-bred, child. Answer your uncle as you should: With great pleasure, Uncle, whenever you wish."

This "With great pleasure, Uncle, whenever you wish" issued almost mechanically from Pepita's faltering lips, then and many times afterward, as she yielded to the admonitions, the speeches, the complaints, and even the imperious commands of her mother.

I see that I am extending myself unduly in telling you

about this Pepita Jiménez and her story; but she interests me and I suppose you, too, for if what they assure me here is true, she is going to be your sister-in-law and my stepmother. I shall try not to linger over details, however, and to give you the gist of things you may know, even though you've been away from here a long time.

Pepita Jiménez married Don Gumersindo.

Envy made her its target during the days preceding the wedding and for some months afterward.

To be sure, the moral aspect of this marriage is highly questionable. But on the girl's side, taking into account her mother's pleas, her complaints, even her command, and bearing in mind that she thought she might in this way provide her mother with a peaceful old age and free her brother from dishonor and infamy by becoming his guardian angel and his provider, it must be admitted that there were extenuating circumstances. At the same time, how can one fathom the intimacies of the heart, the secrets hidden in the mind of a maiden, reared perhaps in an overly sheltered manner and ignorant of everything? How can one say what notions of marriage she might have formed? Perhaps she understood that marrying that old man meant consecrating her life to caring for him, being his nurse, sweetening the last years of his life, not leaving him in solitude and abandonment, in failing health, ministered to by mercenary hands, and illuminating and giving a glow to his final hours through the radiance of her beauty and her youth, like an angel that assumes human form. If something or all of this was in the girl's thoughts, and through her innocence she failed to penetrate other mysteries, the goodness of what she did stands implicit.

Be that as it may, and laying aside these psychological probings which I have no right to make, for I do not know Pepita Jiménez, the fact is that she lived with the old man for three years in heavenly peace. The old fellow seemed happier than ever before; she took care of him and made much of him with admirable solicitude, and during his last and painful illness she waited on him and watched over him with tireless and tender affection. The old man died in her arms, leaving her the heiress to a great fortune.

Although she lost her mother more than two years ago, and has been widowed for more than a year and a half, Pepita still wears her widow's weeds. Her circumspection, her secluded life, and her melancholy are such that anyone might suppose she mourned her husband's death as if he had been in the flower of his youth. There may be those who assume or suspect that Pepita's pride and the certain knowledge she now has of the far-from-poetic means by which she has grown rich gnaw at her conscience and fill her with misgivings; and that, shamed in her own eyes and the eyes of others, she now seeks to console herself and heal the wound in her heart by austerity and retirement.

Here, as elsewhere, people give much thought to money. I am wrong when I say *elsewhere:* in large cities, in the great centers of civilization, there are other honors as much or more sought-after than money, for they open doors and bring esteem and consideration in the world. But in small towns, where neither literary nor scientific fame, nor perhaps distinction of manners, nor elegance, good taste and friendliness in people's dealings with one another are generally valued or understood, there are no other ways of affirming one's social rank than by the money one possesses, or the things that money can buy. Having money, then, and being beautiful in the bargain, and, so everyone says, making good use of her wealth, Pepita finds herself today highly respected and esteemed. The wealthiest young men from this and all the neighboring villages have come to pay court to her. But it would seem that she rejects the most eligible bachelors with great sweetness, trying not to make an enemy of anyone. It is supposed that she has a soul so filled with the most ardent religious faith that her one thought is to devote her life to good works and piety.

They say that Father is no further along and has come out no better than the other suitors; but, in keeping with the old saying that courtesy in no wise detracts from valor, Pepita takes great pains to show the frankest, most affectionate and disinterested friendship for him. She outdoes herself in civility and attentiveness toward him but every time my father tries to speak to her of love, she pulls him up short with a very sweet sermon in which she brings up his past sins and tries to open his eyes to the world and its vanities.

I confess to you that I'm beginning to be curious to meet this woman; I have heard so much about her. I don't believe my curiosity is unjustified. There is nothing vain nor sinful about it; I myself feel as Pepita does; I myself wish that in his advanced years, Father would seek a better life, forget and not stir up the agitation and passions of his youth, and achieve a tranquil, happy, and honored old age. I differ from Pepita in only one thing: I believe that my father can achieve this more easily with a good and worthy woman who loves him than by remaining unmarried. For this reason I wish to make Pepita's acquaintance and see if she may be that woman, for I find this young widow's disdain a little irritating, however affectionate and sweet-spoken she may be. Perhaps a touch of family pride enters into this; if it is wrong, I should like to cast it aside.

If mine were another calling, I should prefer my father to remain unmarried. As an only son, I would be heir to all his wealth, and to the leadership of this village, as we might say; but you well know the firmness of my resolve.

Unworthy and humble though I am, I feel myself called
to the priesthood, and worldly goods make little impression on
my mind. If there is something of the ardor of youth in me
and the vehemence of the passions appropriate to my age, it
shall all be employed in developing a richly abundant charity.
The many books you have given me to read, and my knowledge of the history of the civilizations of the peoples of Asia,
have wedded my intellectual curiosity to the desire to propa-
gate the faith, and invite and stimulate me to go to the Far
East as a missionary. I think that as soon as I leave this village
where you sent me to spend some time with my father, and I
find myself raised to the dignity of the priesthood I shall feel,
ignorant and sinful though I am, that, thanks to the mercy and
the sovereign goodness of the Most High, I have been in-
vested with a divine, undeserved gift—the faculty to pardon
sin and the apostolic mission to teach the people. I believe
that as soon as I receive the perpetual and miraculous grace
of carrying God Himself incarnate in my impure hands I shall
leave Spain and go to distant lands to preach the Gospel.

I am motivated by no vanity whatsoever. I do not think
myself superior to any man. The strength of my faith, the
constancy I feel myself capable of, everything—after the grace
and favor of God—I owe to the wise training, the pious
teachings, and the good example given me by you, my beloved uncle.

I hardly dare confess to myself one thing: but against
my will this thing, this thought, this doubt frequently enters
my mind. Now that it has entered my mind, I wish to confess it to you; I must. It is not right to hide my most hidden
and involuntary thoughts from you. You have taught me to
analyze all that my soul experiences, to seek its origin, good
or evil, to plumb the innermost depths of my heart—in short
to make a scrupulous examination of conscience.

I have often thought about two opposed methods of education: that of those who try to preserve innocence, confusing innocence with ignorance and believing that evil unknown is avoided more easily than that which is known; and the other method, that of those who courageously but with due modesty reveal evil in all its horrible ugliness and all its frightful nakedness to the pupil who has reached the age of reason so that he may abhor and shun it. I am of the opinion that evil must be known if one is to have a better appreciation of infinite, divine goodness. I am grateful to you for having made me know through the milk and honey of your teachings, as the Scripture puts it, all evil and all good, so as to be able to reject the one and aspire to the other with discerning resolution and in full knowledge of the matter. I am glad I am not naive, and that I follow after virtue, and, insofar as it is humanly possible, perfection, fully aware of all the trials, of all the rigors that beset the pilgrim's progress we must make through this vale of tears, and yet not unaware how smooth, how easy, how sweet seems the flowery path that leads to perdition and everlasting death.

Another thing for which I owe you gratitude is the indulgence, the tolerance, not complacent nor lax, but sober and severe, that you knew how to inculcate in me toward the faults and sins of my neighbor.

I say all this to you because I want to speak to you on a matter so delicate, so touchy that I hardly know how to put it into words. In brief, I sometimes ask myself: can this plan of mine be based, at least in part, upon the nature of my relations with my father? Have I really forgiven him in my inmost heart for his conduct toward my poor mother, the victim of his loose living?

I look searchingly into my heart and can find no atom of rancor in it. Quite the contrary. It is filled with gratitude. My father reared me with love; he has tried to honor the memory of my mother in me, and it might be said that in bringing me up, in taking such great pains with me when I was little, he was trying to appease her angry shade, if the shade, the spirit of an angel of goodness and meekness such as she was could be capable of anger. I repeat, then, that I am filled with gratitude toward my father; he acknowledged me, and moreover, when I had reached the age of ten he sent me to you, to whom I owe all that I am.

If there is some seed of virtue in my heart; if there is some glimmering of knowledge in my mind; if there is some honor and good will in my character, I owe it all to you.

My father's affection for me is great; it is extraordinary; the esteem in which he holds me is far beyond my merits. Perhaps vanity may enter into this. There is always something egotistical in fatherly love; it is like a prolongation of the self. All my worth, if I have any, is considered by my father to be his own creation, as though I were an emanation of his personality, in body as well as in spirit. But in any case, I believe he loves me and that in this affection there is an element independent of and superior to all this excusable egotism of which I have spoken.

I feel a great comfort, a great ease in my conscience, and for this I give most fervent thanks to God when I observe and note that the strong ties of blood, Nature's bond, that mysterious link that unites us, leads me to love and revere my father beyond any thought of duty. It would be horrible not to love him like this and to try to force myself to do so in fulfillment of a commandment of God. Yet does my intention to become a priest or friar and not to accept, or to accept only a small part of the ample wealth that will come to me as a legacy and which I can already enjoy during my father's lifetime come (and here lies my doubt) only from my contempt for the things of the world, from a true vocation for the religious life? Or does it spring also from pride, from a hidden rancor, from a grievance, from something in me that does not forgive what my mother forgave with sublime generosity? This doubt assails and torments me at times. But I almost always resolve it in my own favor. I believe that I am not aloof toward my father; I believe that if it were necessary I would accept everything he has, and I pride myself that I am as grateful to him for the little as for the much.

Good-bye, Uncle; henceforth I shall write you often and extensively as you've asked me to, though not at such length as today, to avoid the sin of prolixity.

March 28.

I am getting tired of my stay in this village, and each day I feel a greater desire to go back to you and take Holy Orders. But Father wants to go with me; he wants to be present on that very solemn occasion, and he begs me to remain here with him for two months at least. He is so affable, so affectionate toward me that it would be impossible not to please him in everything. I shall stay here, then, as long as he wishes. To please him I make an effort to enter into things and pretend to enjoy the local diversions; and I go with him to all the outings in the country, and even on hunting trips. I try to appear happier and more animated than I naturally am. As in the village, half in fun, half in praise, they call me the "saint," out of modesty I do my best to conceal any air of saintliness, or to tone it down or humanize it with the virtue of lightheartedness, which was never at odds with saintliness or saints. Nevertheless, I confess that the horseplay and the pastimes, the crude jests and boisterous hilarity wear me out. I should not like to indulge in gossip nor be a slanderer,

even just between you and me and in strictest confidence; but
I often wonder if it might not be a more arduous enterprise
to expound the principles of morality and carry the Gospel
to these people, and more logical and meritorious than to go
to India, Persia, or China, leaving behind so many of my
fellow-countrymen somewhat perverted, if not lost. Who
knows? Some say that modern ideas, materialism, and lack of
faith lie at the root of everything; but if the fault does lie
there, if it has wrought such evil effects, it must be by some
strange, magical, diabolical means, not natural ones, for the
fact is that no one here ever reads a book, good or bad, hence
I cannot even conjecture how they could have been perverted
by the evil doctrines that are rampant today. Can evil doctrine
be in the air, like the miasmas of an epidemic? Perhaps (and
I am sorry to entertain this wicked thought which I mention
only to you), perhaps the clergy itself may be to blame. Is it
fulfilling its mission in Spain? Does it go forth to teach and
inculcate morality among the people? Have those who consecrated themselves to the religious life and to the cure of souls
a true vocation, or is it merely a way of making a living like
any other, with the difference that today only the most
needy, those with the least prospects, the most inept, dedicate
themselves to it, inasmuch as this "career" offers a more
meager future than any other? Be that as it may, the paucity
of educated and virtuous clergymen further whets my desire
to be one. I should not wish to be misled by pride; I recognize
all my defects; but I feel within myself a true calling, and
with divine aid many of my faults may be remedied.

Three days ago we attended the dinner I spoke to you
about at Pepita Jiménez' house. As this woman leads such a
secluded life, I had not met her until the day of the invita-
tion. In truth she seemed to me as pretty as she is reputed to
be, and I noticed that she treats my father with such affability

as to give him some hope, if one may judge by appearances, that in the end she will yield and accept his hand.

As it is possible she may become my stepmother, I observed her at length. She seems to me a strange woman whose moral attributes I cannot gauge with any accuracy. There is a calm about her, an outward peace, which might arise from coldness of soul and heart, from complete command of herself, and from calculating everything while feeling little or nothing. On the other hand, it might come from other qualities in her soul: from a conscience at ease, from the purity of her aspirations and intentions to comply in this life with the duties imposed upon her by society, while keeping higher goals in mind. What is certain is that, either because she is all calculation and never raises her mind to higher spheres, or because she weaves the prose of living and the poetry of her dreams into a harmonious whole, nothing about her strikes a false note in the setting of which she is the center. And yet she has a natural distinction which raises her above and sets her apart from everything around her. She neither affects the local costume nor dresses in city fashion; she blends both styles in her attire so that she looks like a lady, but a village lady. I would judge that she carefully conceals the pains she takes with her appearance. There is no sign of rouge or cosmetics, but the whiteness of her hands, the fingernails so well cared for, and the neatness and daintiness of her dress, bear witness that she gives more thought to these things than a person who lives in a village might be supposed to, than one, moreover, who says that she despises the vanities of the world and thinks only of heavenly matters.

She keeps her house very clean and everything is in perfect order. The furnishings are not artistic nor elegant, but neither is there anything pretentious or in bad taste about them. A multitude of flowers and plants lend poetry to her dwelling, both in the patio and in the highways. To be sure she has no rare plant nor exotic flower; but her plants and flowers, of the commonest varieties around here, give evidence of loving attention.

Several canaries in gilt cages enliven the whole house with their trilling. It is apparent that their mistress needs living creatures on which to lavish affection; and besides several maid-servants, who must have been chosen with care, for it cannot be mere chance that they are all pretty, she has like elderly spinsters, various animals to keep her company: a parrot, a fluffy, well-washed little female spaniel, and two or three cats so gentle and friendly that they climb all over one.

At one end of the main parlor there is a kind of prie-dieu where a Christ Child, carved in wood, painted red and white, blue-eyed, and very handsome, is enshrined. His dress is of white satin, with a blue cloak, starred in gold, and he is all covered with trinkets and jewels. The little altar where the Christ Child stands is decorated with flowers and around it are pots of broom and laurel. On the altar itself, which has steps or little stairs, many candles burn.

I do not know what to think after seeing all this, but frequently I'm inclined to believe that the widow loves herself most of all, that she keeps her cats, her canaries, her flowers, and even the Christ Child for her own amusement and as an outlet for this love, and that as far as her soul is concerned, she may not be much above the canaries and the cats.

It cannot be denied that Pepita Jiménez is discreet; she voiced no foolish jest, no impertinent question regarding my vocation and the holy orders I am about to take. She talked to me about local affairs, about farming, about the last vintage and the olive harvest, and how to improve the process of wine-making—all this with modesty and naturalness, never trying to pass herself off as an authority.

My father was politeness itself; he seemed rejuvenated, and his marked attentiveness toward the lady of his thoughts was received with graciousness, if not with love.

The doctor, the notary, and the Vicar—a great family friend and Pepita's spiritual father—were among the guests.

The Vicar must hold a high opinion of her, for several times he spoke to me privately of her charity, of her many gifts to the poor, of her compassion and goodness to everyone. In short, he told me she is a saint.

Having heard the Vicar, and having confidence in his judgment, I can only wish that my father and Pepita would marry. As Father is not cut out for a penitential life, this would be the only manner in which he might mend his ways, hitherto so restless and stormy, and finally achieve an orderly and peaceful, if not exemplary, end.

When we left the house of Pepita Jiménez and returned to our own, Father talked to me openly of his plans. He told me he had been quite a rake, that he had led a very wicked life and could not see how he could mend his ways, despite his years, unless that woman, his salvation, would return his love and marry him. Taking for granted that she was going to love and marry him, Father spoke to me of practical matters. He told me he was very rich and that he would leave me the lion's share of his wealth, even though he might have other children. I replied that I needed very little money for my plans and aims in life, and that my greatest pleasure would be to see him happy with a wife and children, his old dissipations forgotten. Then my father spoke to me of his amorous aspirations with such frankness and animation that you would have said I was the father and he a boy my age or younger. To impress me with the desirability of his sweetheart and the difficulty of his triumph, he cited the situation and the eligibility of the fifteen or twenty suitors Pepita had had, all of whom she had rejected. As for himself, she had rejected him, too, up to a point, but he flattered himself that her final word had not been spoken, for Pepita singled him out so markedly and demonstrated such great affection for him that, if it wasn't love, it could easily be converted into love by association and in view of his unswerving adoration. Moreover, in my father's opinion, there was some fantastic element of sophistry in Pepita's indifference which could be overcome in the end. Pepita had no wish to withdraw to a convent, nor was she inclined to the penitential life. In spite of her retirement and religious devotion, it was plain to be seen that she delighted in pleasing. The neatness and care of her person had nothing in it of the recluse. The cause of Pepita's indifference, said my father, undoubtedly lay in her pride, justified in the main. She was naturally elegant, distinguished; she was a superior being, thanks to her will and her intelligence, however modest she might feign to be. How then could she yield her heart to the rustics who up to now had laid siege to it? She fancied that her soul was filled with a mystical love of God, and that she could be satisfied with God alone, for as yet no mortal clever and acceptable enough to make her forget even her Infant Jesus had crossed her path. "Though it may be immodest of me, I flatter myself that I shall yet be that lucky mortal," Father added.

These, dear Uncle, are the preoccupations and occupations of my father in this village, and these are the matters (so foreign to me, and alien to my plans and thoughts) that he frequently discusses with me, and about which he wants my opinion.

It would seem that your excessive indulgence toward

me has given me the reputation of a man of judgment. I pass
here for a fount of knowledge; everyone brings me his troubles
and asks me to show him the way he ought to follow. The
good Vicar himself, even at the risk of revealing some of the
secrets of the confessional, has now come to consult me about
various problems of conscience that have been raised in the
confession box.

One of these cases, referred to me in the greatest confidence, like all the others, and without revealing the name of
the person in question, has aroused my interest. He tells me
that one of his daughters in confession suffers great doubts
because she feels drawn toward the solitary and contemplative
life by an irresistible compulsion; but at times she fears that
this fervor is not accompanied by a true humility but that in
part the very demon of pride impels and motivates her.

To love God above all things, to seek Him where he
abides in the core of the soul, to purify one's self of all passions
and earthly affections so as to be united with Him, are truly
pious desires and good resolutions; but the doubt lies in finding out, in determining whether or not they are born of an
exaggerated self-love. This penitent seems to ask herself
whether, sinful and unworthy though she be, she is assuming
that her soul is of greater worth than those of her fellow-
beings and that the inner beauty of her mind and will might
be disturbed and clouded by the affection of creatures whom
she knows and considers beneath her. "Do I love God," she asks,
"not merely above all things and infinitely, but above what I
disdain and reject, which cannot fill my heart? If this is the
basis of my devotion, there are two great flaws in it: first, that
it does not rest upon a pure love of God, full of humility and
charity, but on pride instead; and second, that this devotion is
not firm and authentic, but a thing of air. For who can be certain that his soul may not forget the love of its Creator when

that love is not infinite, arising instead from the fact that there is no living creature whom it judges worthy of the soul's whole love?"

The Vicar came to consult me about this problem of conscience, an extremely involved and subtle one to be worrying a village woman. I have tried to avoid saying anything, alleging my inexperience and my youth, but the Vicar persisted so that I could not help giving thought to the case. I said, and I should be very pleased if you were to approve of my opinion, that the important thing for this troubled daughter in confession would be to look with greater benevolence upon the men around her, and instead of analyzing and laying bare their faults with the scalpel of criticism, she should try to cover them with the mantle of charity, bringing to light all their good qualities and weighing them carefully so as to be able to love and esteem them; that she should force herself to see in every human being an object worthy of love, a true neighbor, an equal, a soul in whose depths lies a treasure of fine qualities and virtues—a creature, in short, made in the image and likeness of God. By thus elevating all that surrounds us, loving and valuing all creatures at their true worth and at even more than their true worth, trying not to hold ourselves above them in anything, but rather examining sincerely our own conscience in order to discover all our faults and sins and thus gaining a blessed humility and forgetfulness of self, the heart will be filled with human affection and will not despise, but rather esteem highly the worth of all things and all persons. Then if divine love rises with invincible might upon this foundation, there can be no fear that love is born of an exaggerated self-esteem, of pride, or an unjust disdain for one's neighbor, for it will be born of a pure and saintly regard for infinite goodness and beauty.

If, as I suspect, it is Pepita Jiménez who consulted the

Vicar regarding these doubts and distresses, it seems to me that my father cannot flatter himself as yet that he is greatly loved; but, if the Vicar succeeds in giving her my advice, and she accepts it and puts it into practice, either she will become a Mary of Agreda,[3] or something similar, or, what is more likely, she will lay aside mysticism and coldness, and will be willing and content to accept the hand and heart of my father, who is in no way her inferior.

April 4.

The monotony of my life in this village is beginning to bore me a great deal, not because I was more active elsewhere; quite the contrary. Here I walk a lot, or ride horseback. To please my father, I go to the country and appear at clubs and meetings. In short, I live as though estranged from myself and my own kind. My intellectual life is nil; I never open a book and I am left hardly a moment to think and meditate in peace. As the pleasure of my way of life derived from such thought and meditation, what I am doing now seems to me monotonous. Thanks to the patience you counselled for every occasion, I can endure it.

Another reason that my mind is not entirely at rest is the desire, stronger each day, to assume the status upon which I've ben resolved for years now. At this moment, it seems to me that it is like a profanation to let my mind stray to other matters when the realization of the abiding dream of my life lies so near. This idea haunts me and I ponder it so frequently that today I am filled with wonder at the beauty of all created things—the sky so full of stars on these calm spring nights in

[3] *María Fernández Coronel* (1602-1665), *Abbess of Agreda, a Navarese convent of Franciscan nuns; author of mystical books; correspondent and adviser of Philip IV.*

this part of Andalusia; these gracious fields now covered with growing plants, these cool, pleasant gardens with their beautiful, shady nooks, the gentle brooks and ponds, the many secret retreats, the warbling birds, the flowers and fragant herbs. This wonder and this exaltation of soul which used to arise in me solely from the religious emotion that filled me, stimulating and ennobling rather than weakening me, today seem almost sinful distractions, an unpardonable forgetting of the eternal for the temporal, of the divine and supersensory for the sensory. Though I make small progress in virtue, though my spirit is never free from the phantasms of the mind, though I never liberate the inner man from external impressions and from the tiresome processes of thought, though incapable through an act of love of concentrating on the core of simple intelligence, there to find truth and goodness at the apex of the mind, freed from form and imagery, I assure you that I fear the imaginary manner of prayer that befits a man so unlearned and so fleshy as I. I am even distrustful of rational meditation: I don't want to know God through reason, nor love him by citing the grounds for love. I should like to launch myself into intimate, spiritual contemplation at one thrust. Oh, for the wings of a dove that I might fly to the breast of my soul's Master! But what and where are my merits? Where the mortifications, the prayerful vigils, and the fasts? What have I done, Oh my God, that thou shouldst be mindful of me?

I know full well that today godless people baselessly accuse our holy religion of inciting the soul to abhor all worldly things, to despise and disdain Nature, perhaps even to fear her, as though she were imbued with something diabolical, concentrating all their love and affection on what they call the monstrous egotism of loving God, for they believe that in loving Him the soul loves itself. I know full well that this is not the true doctrine; divine love is charity, and to love God is to love all things, for all things are in God, and God is in all things in His divine and ineffable fashion. I know full well that I do not sin in loving all things for the love of God, that is, in loving them rightly for themselves, for what are they but the manifestations, the artifacts of God's love? And yet, I know not what strange fear, what curious scruple, what barely perceptible and indeterminate remorse now torments me whenever I feel, as in the days of my childhood, my youth, a welling up of tenderness, a kind of rapture, upon entering a leafy bower, hearing the song of the nightingale in the silence of the night, listening to the twitter of the swallows and the amorous cooing of the turtledove, or looking at flowers, or watching the stars. Sometimes I fancy that there is a trace of sensual delight in all this, something that makes me forget, for a moment at least, higher aspirations. I don't want my spirit to sin against the flesh; but neither do I want to be distracted by material beauty from the contemplation of greater beauty, nor permit even the most delicate, subtle, and ethereal delights, such as the thin whistle of cool air laden with country scents, the song of the birds, the majestic and reposeful silence of the night hours in these gardens and orchards, perceived though they be through the spirit more than the flesh, to cool even for a moment my love for Him who created this harmonious fabric of the world.

I am not unaware that all these material things are like the print of a book, symbols and characters whereby the soul through study may discover a deep meaning, and may read and see disclosed the beauty of God. But it is an imperfect transcription, a code as it were, for these things represent but do not portray it. At times I fall back upon this distinction to fortify my scruples and to mortify myself. For if I love the beauty of earthly things as they are, I tell myself, and if I love that beauty to excess, that is idolatry. I must love beauty as a symbol, a representation of a hidden and divine beauty which is worth a thousand times more in every way, and incomparably superior.

My twenty-second birthday came a few days ago. Until now my religious fervor has been such that I have experienced no love other than the immaculate love for God Himself and His holy religion. I long to spread it abroad and see it triumphant in every corner of the earth. But I confess that some profane feeling has been mingled with this pure affection. You know it; I have told you so a thousand times. And you have replied, with your usual indulgent regard for me, that a man is not an angel, and that merely to aspire to such perfection is pride; that I must subdue these feelings, not seek to smother them entirely. To love learning, to seek acclaim, even to form a not unflattering concept of oneself—all this, in moderation, doubtless has something selfish in it, though scrutinized and mitigated with Christian humility and directed always to a good end. But it may serve as a spur and a prop to the firmest and noblest resolutions. The scruple assailing me today, then, comes not from pride or over-confidence, from a thirst for worldly glory, or excessive intellectual curiosity. It is nothing related to egotism; in a sense it is the contrary. I feel a kind of lassitude, a debility, a weakness of the will, too great a tendency to tears. I weep so easily from tenderness at seeing a lovely little flower or contemplating the mysterious, tenuous, and slender ray from a remote star that it almost frightens me.

Tell me what you think of all this, whether there is some ailment of the soul in this inclination.

April 8

The rustic amusements go on and I have to take part in them, much against my will.

I have gone with Father to look at almost all his farms; he and his friends are astounded that I am not wholly ignorant of all rural matters. It seems to them that the study of theology is at odds with all knowledge of natural things. How they admire my erudition when they see I can distinguish one variety of grape from another, the Pedro-Jiménez vine-stalk from the ordinary, and from the Don-Bueno, at the period when they are barely sending forth new tendrils! How they have marvelled, too, that I can distinguish barley from wheat, and anise from beans when they are just sprouting; that I recognize many fruit and shade trees and I can even identify the grasses that spring up of themselves in the field and can cite their various properties and virtues!

Pepita Jiménez learned from my father how much I like the gardens hereabouts and has invited us to see one she owns a short distance from the village and to feast on the early strawberries that grow there. This eagerness of Pepita's to lavish so much attention on Father, who courts her and whom she rebuffs, at times seems to me to have a touch of coquetry about it, something blameworthy. But later when I see Pepita and find her so natural, so serene, and so unaffected, the evil thought leaves me and I believe she does everything guilelessly and has no other purpose than to preserve the friendship that binds her to my family.

Be that as it may, we went to the garden with Pepita on the afternoon of the day before yesterday. It is a beautiful spot, the most pleasant and picturesque you can imagine. The little stream irrigating almost all these gardens flows alongside the one we were visiting, feeding a thousand ditches. At that point it forms a dam, and when the excess irrigation water is released, it falls into a deep ravine covered on each bank with white and black poplars, osiers, oleanders in bloom, and other leafy trees. The clean transparent cascade spreads out at the base, sending up spray, then follows its winding course through a bed that Nature has dug, its banks adorned with a thousand grasses and flowers and at this season, with carpets of violets. The slopes at one end of the garden are covered with walnut, fig, hazelnut, and other fruit and nut trees. Plots of vegetables, strawberries, tomatoes, potatoes, beans, and peppers are planted on the level ground as well as a small flower garden, with a great profusion of the flowers most commonly grown here, especially roses, of which there are a thousand varieties. The gardener's cottage is much prettier and cleaner than most, and alongside it another small building is reserved for the owner. There Pepita regaled us with a splendid little luncheon including strawberries, which were the reason for our visit to that place. There was an abundance of them for that early in the season, and we ate them with milk from the goats that Pepita also raises there.

The doctor, the notary, my aunt, Doña Casilda, my father, and I were all present at this outing; and, of course, the Vicar, the spiritual father of Pepita and more than that, the admirer and perpetual singer of her praises.

It was not the gardener, nor his wife, nor the gardener's small boy, nor any other peasant who served us our lunch, but as a touch of refinement two beautiful girls, Pepita's maids and, so to speak, her confidantes, dressed in country attire though with consummate daintiness and elegance. They wore bright-colored percale dresses, short and tight-fitting, their shoulders covered with silk kerchiefs, their heads bare, their thick, glossy black hair braided and then tied in a knot shaped like a hammer, and in front curls fastened with hairpins called in this region snails. Each of the girls had a spray of fresh roses tucked into the knot, or chignon.

Except that it was of richer material and black, Pepita's dress was just as rustic as theirs. Her merino gown was in the same style as the maids', and though not short, it did not drag on the ground and sweep up the country dust. A modest little kerchief of black silk covered her shoulders and bosom, in the local style. On her head she wore no coif, flower, jewel, or ornament other than her own blonde hair. I noticed in Pepita only one touch of a certain studied refinement. She departed from village custom in wearing gloves. It is apparent that she takes great care of her hands, and perhaps she shows a measure of vanity in keeping them very white and pretty, with shining, rosy nails. But this is an excusable human weakness. After all, if memory serves, Saint Teresa[4] shared that vanity when she was young, but that did not keep her from becoming so great a saint.

Indeed I can explain to myself this sly vanity, though I do not excuse it. It is so distinguished, so aristocratic, to have beautiful hands! At times I even imagine there is something symbolic about it. The hand is the instrument of our works, the token of our nobility, the means intelligence employs to give form to its artistic thoughts, endowing the creations of the will with life, and exercising the empire God granted to man over all creatures. The rough, nervous, strong, perhaps calloused hand of a worker nobly reveals power in an active and mechanical way. Pepita's hands, on the contrary, are almost as translucent as alabaster, slightly tinged with pink where, one fancies, the pure and subtle blood is visibly circulating, lending the veins a light touch of blue. These hands, I say, slender-fingered and peerlessly modeled, seem the symbols of the magical empire, the mysterious dominion possessed and exercised without material force by the human spirit over all tangible things that have come without material force from the hand of God and which He completes and betters through the

---

[4] *Teresa of Avila (1515-1582), founder with St. John of the Cross of the Discalced Order of Carmelite nuns, a great administrator, mystical writer and poet. Canonized in 1622.*

medium of man. It seems impossible that anyone with hands
like Pepita's should harbor an impure thought, a gross idea, a
base plan discordant with the clean hands that would have
to carry it out.

Needless to say, my father showed himself as charmed as
ever with Pepita and she as considerate and affectionate as ever
toward him, though her affection was perhaps more filial than
Father might have wished. Despite his reputation for behaving
as a rule with slight respect toward women and for being somewhat coarse around them, the truth is that my father treats
this one with such respect and deference that Amadis[5] could
never have outdone him during the lowest-keyed phase of his
wooing of the Lady Oriana. Never a jarring word, never an
inopportune gallantry, never an amorous jest like those the
Andalusians so often permit themselves. Father hardly dares say
to Pepita: "What lovely eyes you have." And the fact is that
if he were to say it, he would not be lying, for hers are large
and as green, beautiful, and well-shaped as Circe's.[6] What lends
them greater beauty and enchantment is that she seems not to
know it, for she shows not the slightest intention to please or
attract anyone with the sweetness of her glances. You might
say she thinks eyes were made to see with and nothing more.
From what I have heard, I assume the contrary—that most
young and pretty women make of their eyes a weapon like an
electrical instrument or a bolt of lighting to conquer and captivate hearts. Truly Pepita's eyes are not like that; there is
serenity and a heavenly peace in them. Not that they could be
said to gaze forth with cold indifference. Her eyes are full of
compassion and sweetness. They rest with affection on a ray of

---

[5] *Amadis, hero of the Spanish epic* Amadis de Gaula, *c. 1496, novel
of chivalry, beloved by Don Quixote. Oriana, his lady, was the daughter
of the king of Greece. Amadis won her after a series of ordeals.*

[6] *Circe, daughter of the sun, the sorceress who turned Ulysses' men
into swine.*

light, a flower, any inanimate object; and on her fellow beings with a feeling that is even gentler, more humane and benign. But never, however young, gallant, and daring these may be, does she give them grounds to assume that in that serene and tranquil gaze lies anything more than charity and neighborly love, or at most, a friendly inclination.

I pause to ask myself whether all this is studied, whether Pepita is a great actress; but the acting would have to be so perfect and so well concealed that it seems impossible. It is nature herself that sets the norm, then, and guides this look and those eyes. No doubt Pepita loved her mother first, and later, circumstances led her to love Don Gumersindo out of duty, as her life's companion. Such passions as any earthly object might inspire were probably thus quenched in her and she loves God and all things for the love of God. Perhaps she finds herself in a peaceful and even enviable spiritual state where if anything blameworthy exists, it might be selfishness of which she herself is not aware. It is very comfortable to feel affection in this even-tenored way, without the torments of love; to have no passions to fight; to make of one's love and affection for others an extension and a complement, as it were, of self-love.

Sometimes I ask myself whether, in mentally censuring Pepita's state, it is not I myself whom I am censuring. What do I know about what goes on in the soul of that woman that I should censure her? In thinking that I can see into her soul, may I not be looking into mine? Thanks to your wise teaching, I have no passion for conquest, and never have had. All my well-directed inclinations, all my instincts, good or bad, move toward the same end with no obstacles nor stumbling-blocks. Not only shall my noble and disinterested desires be achieved in gaining that end, but my selfish ones, too: the pursuit of glory, the desire for knowledge, my curiosity to visit distant lands, my zeal to win name and fame. All this adds up to the attainment of the career I have understaken. Sometimes it occurs to me that in this respect I am more to be blamed than Pepita, even assuming that she is to be blamed at all.

I have already taken minor orders; I have stripped my soul of the vanities of the world; I am tonsured; I have prostrated myself before the altar, and yet a future filled with ambition lies before my eyes, and I see with pleasure that I can attain it, and flatter myself that my qualifications for it are steadfast and worthy, however much I call upon modesty to avoid over-confidence. On the other hand, to what does this woman aspire, what does she want? I criticize her because she takes care of her hands, because perhaps she views her beauty with complacency; I almost censure that beauty, the neatness of her attire, a subtle hint of coquetry in the very modesty and simplicity with which she dresses. Well, then, must virtue be slovenly? Must sanctity be dirty? Cannot a pure, clean soul take pleasure in a clean body? This uncharitable view I take of Pepita's daintiness and neatness is a strange quirk. Can it be because she may be my stepmother? But suppose she doesn't want to be my stepmother! What if she doesn't love my father! Certainly women are odd. Who knows but that in the bottom of her heart she doesn't want to love and marry my father? Or perhaps, in keeping with the old saw that you judge the worth of a thing by what it costs you, she may propose (forgive me the expression) to goad him with her disdain, keep him dancing attendance on her, put the constancy of his affection to the test and in the end calmly say yes. Well, we shall see!

The fact is that the party in the garden was mildly festive. We talked about flowers, fruit, grafting, planting, and a thousand other things relating to farm work. Pepita displayed her knowledge of agronomy in competition with my father, myself and the Vicar, whose mouth fell open every time she spoke, and who swears that in all the seventy-odd years of his life, in all the pilgrimages that have taken him over most of Andalusia, he has never known a woman more circumspect or more exact in everything she thinks and says.

When we come home after one of these expeditions, I repeat to Father insistently that I want to go back to you so as to hasten the longed-for moment when I shall be raised to the priesthood. But Father is so happy to have me at his side, and he so enjoys it here in the village, looking after his farms, exercising his all-embracing prerogatives as political leader, adoring Pepita and consulting her in everything as if she were his nymph Egeria,[7] that he always finds and will continue to find, perhaps for several months, some valid pretext to keep me here. One day he has to clarify the wine in I don't know how many casks; next he has to decant other casks; now he has to plow the vineyards again; next to cultivate the olive groves. In short, he holds me here against my wishes, though I shouldn't say against my wishes, for I consider it a blessing to live with a father who is so good to me.

The worst of it is that I am afraid of becoming too materialistic from living this life. It seems to me I feel a sort of dryness of spirit during prayer; my religious fervor is diminishing; the world keeps penetrating and infiltrating my character. I suffer distractions while praying; in my solitude when my soul should be lifted up to God, I don't pay the profound attention I used to pay to what I am saying. On the contrary, the tenderness of my heart, not fixed on any suitable object, not employed and consumed as it should be, gushes forth and at times floods over objects and circumstances that are puerile, that seem to me ridiculous, and that I am ashamed of. If I awaken in the silence of deep night and hear some enamored rustic, accom-

---

[7] *Egeria, nymph of the fountain, who taught the Roman king, Numa, the lessons in law later embodied in the Roman Code.*

panied by his poorly played guitar, singing a couplet from a fandango or a rondo, neither apt, poetic, nor delicate, I melt as though I were listening to the most celestial melody. A mad, senseless compassion comes over me at times. The other day the children of Father's wheelwright robbed a sparrow's nest and when I saw the naked little birds violently wrenched from their loving mother, I felt acute anguish and I must confess that tears came to my eyes. A few days earlier, a farmer brought a little calf with a broken leg in from the country. He was taking it to the butcher and had come to ask Father what part of it he would like for the table. Father asked for several pounds of meat, the head, and the feet. I was so moved at seeing the calf that I was on the point of buying it from the man to see if I could heal it and keep it alive, but shame kept me from it. In short, dear uncle, it is only because of the great confidence I have in you that I tell you these instances of a vague and exaggerated sentimentality in the hope that you will see from them that I need to go back to my old life, to my studies, to my lofty speculations and become a priest in order to feed with the good, solid fuel that it ought to have this fire that is devouring my soul.

April 14.

I go on living the same life as ever, kept here by my father's pleas.

My greatest pleasure, next to living with him, is the companionship and conversation of the Vicar, in whose company I often take long walks. It hardly seems possible that a man of his age, surely close to eighty, can be so strong, so agile, and such a good walker. I tire before he does, and there is no untrodden way, no wild spot, no craggy hilltop in this vicinity that we have not visited.

More and more the Vicar reconciles me to the Spanish clergy whom I have sometimes criticized for their lack of learning when talking with you. I often say to myself how much more worthwhile this man is, so affectionate and innocent, so full of candor and good will, than some well-read person whose soul does not glow, as his does, with the fire of charity and the purest and most sincere faith. Don't think the Vicar's mind is commonplace. It is untutored, but quick and lucid. Sometimes I fancy that my good opinion of him may arise from the attention with which he listens to me, yet it does seem to me that he grasps everything with remarkable acuity and that he must combine a deep love for our holy religion with an appreciation of all the good things that modern civilization has brought us. The simplicity, the eschewing demonstrations of exaggerated sentimentality, in short, the naturalness of the Vicar's exercise of the most burdensome acts of charity particularly charm me. There is no misfortune he does not remedy, no unfortunate he does not console, no humiliation he does not try to undo, no penury he does not hasten to remedy.

Admittedly, he finds in Pepita Jiménez a potent helper in all this. He is forever praising to the skies her devotion and her compassionate nature.

This near-worship the Vicar renders to Pepita is substantiated by, and almost goes hand in hand with, her thousand good works; almsgiving, prayer, public worship, and the care of the needy. Pepita does not give to the poor alone; she also donates for novenas, sermons, and church feasts. Whenever the parish altars gleam with beautiful flowers, Pepita's generosity can be thanked, for she sends them from her garden. If today the Virgin of Sorrows displays a resplendent new silver-embroidered black velvet mantle which replaces the old, worn-out one, Pepita has paid for it. The Vicar keeps pointing out and eternally praising these and her other good works. So when

I am not talking about my own plans, my vocation, my studies (topics that delight the Vicar and keep him hanging on my words), after a thousand twists and turns the conversation with him always comes around to Pepita Jiménez. But after all, whom else can the Vicar talk about? His companionship with the doctor, the druggist, the wealthy farmers of the vicinity can provide scarcely enough material for three words of conversation. As the Vicar possesses the quality, rare in a villager, of disliking gossip about other people's lives, of declining to broadcast scandal, he has no one to talk about but the woman in question whom he often visits. From what he says one may infer that he carries on the most intimate conversations with her.

I don't know how much Pepita Jiménez has read, nor what schooling she has had, but judging by what the Vicar tells me, she must be endowed with a restless and inquiring spirit, which gives rise to an infinite number of questions and problems she is eager to clarify and resolve, and she lays them before the Vicar, leaving him gratified and confused. This man, with a rustic upbringing, a run-of-the-mill priest, to use the vulgar phrase, has a mind open to every ray of truth, though lacking initiative. Apparently the problems and questions that Pepita propounds to him open up new horizons and new roads, albeit nebulous and ill-defined, which he never even dreamed of, and cannot wholly clarify, though he is enchanted by their vagueness, novelty, and mystery.

The Vicar is not unaware that this is dangerous ground, and that he and Pepita are running the risk of a fall into some heresy all unawares. But he reassures himself, for he knows his Catechism by heart, though far from being a great theologian. He trusts in God to show him the way; he hopes not to go astray, and is sure that Pepita will follow his counsel and never lose her way.

So the two of them construct a thousand poetic fancies,

beautiful though formless, concerning all the mysteries of our religion and the articles of our faith. They cherish a deep devotion to the Blessed Virgin Mary, Our Lady, and I am fascinated to see how they manage to weave together the popular idea or concept of the Virgin with some of the most recondite theological hypotheses.

From what the Vicar tells me, I can see that for all her outward calm and serenity her soul has been pierced by a sharp barb of sorrow. She has a love of purity that is contradicted by her past. Pepita was fond of Don Gumersindo as her companion, her benefactor, the man to whom she owes everything; but the memory of him as her husband torments and shames her.

Her devotion to the Virgin reveals that the memory of her unworthy and sterile marriage has left in her mind a feeling of painful humiliation and gnawing melancholy.

Even in her adoration for the Infant Jesus, represented by the lovely carved image in her house, a frustrated mother-love is interposed, a mother-love that seeks its object in a creature born without sin or impurity.

The Vicar says Pepita adores the Infant Jesus as her God, but loves him with the same maternal love she would feel for a son, if she had one, and if there were nothing in his conception to feel ashamed of. The Vicar notices that when she prays to the Blessed Virgin and cares for her beautiful carved Child Jesus, she is dreaming of the ideal mother and the ideal son, both immaculate.

I assure you I don't know what to make of such idiosyncrasies. I know so little about women! What the Vicar tells me about Pepita surprises me. Indeed when I think, as I do more and more, that Pepita is good, not bad, a certain terror for my father comes over me at times. I believe that for all his fifty-five years, he is in love, and though Pepita is good by intention, she may, without premeditation or calculation on her part, be an instrument of the spirit of evil. She may possess an unknowing and instinctive coquetry, more invincible, effective and dangerous even, than that which is born of premeditation, calculation, and reason.

At times I say to myself: Who knows but that in spite of Pepita's good works, her prayers, her secluded and devout life, her alms and donations to the churches, all that lies behind the Vicar's affection for her, there may not be a worldly spell, a trace of black magic in this prestige she surrounds herself with, which leaves this simple Vicar bemused, putty in her hands, thinking and talking constantly of her?

The very ascendency that Pepita exercises over a man as skeptical as my father, over such a virile and unsentimental nature, is indeed strange.

Neither can Pepita's good works explain the widespread respect and affection she arouses in these rustics. Little children flock to see her on the few occasions when she goes out into the street, and want to kiss her hand. Young girls smile at her and greet her affectionately. All the men take off their hats as she passes by, and bow with spontaneous reverence and the most simple and natural admiration for her.

Pepita Jiménez, whom many have known from birth, whom all knew in her poverty while she lived with her mother, and whom they later saw married to the decrepit and miserly Don Gumersindo, has made everyone forget all this. She seems like a pilgrim from some distant land, from some higher, purer, more radiant sphere, arousing and moving all her fellow-citizens to an affectionate respect and a kind of loving admiration.

I see that unawares I have been falling into the fault I have been criticizing in the Vicar, that I talk to you about nothing but Pepita Jiménez. But it is only natural, for no one talks about anything else here. The village seems to be filled with the spirit, the thought, the image of this singular woman, whom I have not yet been able to prove either an angel or a subtle coquette full of *instinctive shrewdness,* though the terms seem contradictory. The truth is that in all conscience I am becoming convinced that this woman is not a coquette and does not dream of ensnaring the will of others to satisfy her vanity.

Pepita Jiménez possesses both sincerity and candor. To see her is to believe that. Her light, reposeful walk, her slender form, her smooth, clear brow, the soft, pure light of her glance, all blend in a concerted rhythm in perfect harmony unmarred by a discordant note.

How sorry I am that I came here and have stayed such a long time! If I had stayed in your house and in the Seminary, I never would have seen nor had anything to do with anyone but my companions and teachers; I would have known nothing of the world except through speculation and theory. Now suddenly I find myself thrown into the world, even though it be only a village, and distracted from my studies, meditations, and prayers by a thousand profane things.

April 20.

Your latest letters have brought welcome comfort to my soul, my dearest Uncle. Benevolent as ever, you admonish and enlighten me with discreet and useful warnings.

You are right: my vehemence deserves reproof. I *do* want to achieve the end without supplying the means; I *do* want to come to the end of the journey without first walking the rough road step by step.

I complain of aridity of the spirit during prayer, of being distracted, of dissipating my tenderness on puerile things. I

long to fly to the intimate company of God, to contemplation
of the essential, while neglecting inward prayer and rational
and reasonable meditation. Unless I can achieve purity, unless
I see the light, how can I achieve the delight of love?

There is great arrogance in me, and I must try to humble
myself in my own eyes so that the spirit of evil may not humble
me, God so willing, as punishment for my presumption and
my pride.

Yet in spite of everything, I think it would not be as easy
as your warning implies for me to suffer an ugly, unpremeditated fall. My trust is not in myself, but in the mercy of God
and His grace, and I hope that it may never come to pass.

You are more than right, nevertheless, in counselling me
not to let myself be linked in too close a friendship with Pepita
Jiménez; but this is far from being the case.

I am not unaware that men of God and the saints, who
must serve as our example and model, have achieved with
women a relationship of close familiarity and love only in their
old age, or after they had been well tested and broken through
penance, or when there was a great disparity of age between
them and their pious friends, as in the case of Saint Jerome
and Saint Paula;[8] of Saint John of the Cross[9] and Saint Teresa.
Yet even so, though their love was spiritual in every sense, I
know that a man may sin through excess. For God alone must
fill our soul, as its lord and spouse. Any other being who dwells
within the soul may do so only in the capacity of friend, slave,
or handmaiden of the Spouse, and whom the Spouse finds
pleasing.

---

[8] *St. Jerome (c. 340-420), scholar and teacher, author of the Latin
translation of the Scriptures known as the Vulgate. He travelled with
St. Paula and her daughter, rich Roman ladies, and together they
founded four convents, three of them for nuns, in Bethlehem.*

[9] *St. John of the Cross (1542-1591), greatest of Spanish mystic
poets. He was guided by St. Teresa in his life of devotion. Canonized in
1726.*

Do not think, then, that I am boasting of my invincibility and that I scorn the dangers, and challenge them, and seek them. He who lives by the sword shall perish by the sword. And if the Prophet King, David, so close to the heart of the Lord and so much His favorite, and Solomon, despite the supernatural wisdom implanted in him by God, were tempted and sinned, because God had turned His face from them, what may I not fear, miserable sinner that I am, so untutored in the snares of the devil, and so weak and unskilled in the struggle for virtue?

Filled as I am with the salutary fear of God and duly mistrustful of my own weakness, I shall not forget your advice and your prudent admonitions. I shall fervently pray and meditate on divine matters so as to abhor what is to be abhorred in worldly things; but I assure you that up to now, however deeply I examine my conscience and however jealously I probe its most hidden corners, I can find nothing to make me fear what you fear.

If my earlier letters can be summed up as encomiums to the soul of Pepita Jiménez, it is the fault of my father and the Vicar, not mine, for in the beginning, far from favoring this woman, I was unjustly prejudiced against her.

As for Pepita's physical beauty and grace, believe me I have observed all that with complete purity of mind. And though it hurts me to say so, though I may wound you a little, I must confess that if some slight stain has come to blur the limpid mirror of my soul that gives back the image of Pepita, your harsh suspicion, which has almost brought me for a moment to suspect myself, is the cause.

But no. What have I thought, what have I gazed upon, what have I praised in Pepita that could lead anyone to infer that I tend to feel for her anything but friendship and that innocent admiration that a work of art can inspire, and particularly if it is the work of the sovereign Artificer, and nothing less than His temple?

In any case, dear Uncle, I have to live in the world; I have to deal with people; I have to see them, and I am not going to pluck out my eyes. You yourself have told me a thousand times that you'd like me to lead an active life, preaching the divine word, spreading it throughout the world, and not dedicate myself to the contemplative life in solitude and isolation. Well then, if this is the case, as indeed it is, how am I to conduct myself so as not to see Pepita Jiménez? Either I make myself ridiculous by closing my eyes in her presence, or I have to see and notice that beauty of hers, the pink and white clarity of her skin, the evenness and pearly whiteness of her teeth, which she shows when she smiles, the fresh carmine of her lips, the smoothness and serenity of her brow, and a thousand other attractions that God has given her. To be sure, in a man who carries the seed of licentious thoughts in his soul, each of the impressions Pepita produces might be like the meeting of flint and steel, kindling the spark that ignites and devours everything. But forewarned as I am against this danger, guarded and shielded by Christian prudence, I do not think I have anything to fear. Moreover, though it is rash to seek danger, it is cowardly not to know how to face it, to flee from it when it confronts us.

Never doubt that I see in Pepita Jiménez a beautiful child of God, and as a sister in God I love her. If I feel a certain predilection for her, it can be traced to the praise of her I hear from my father, the Vicar, and almost everyone in this village.

I wish, for my father's sake, that Pepita would lay aside her plans and thoughts for a retired life and would marry him. But barring that, I should be glad if Pepita remained steadfast in her chaste widowhood, if I were sure that my father feels only a passing fancy and not a true love for her. And when I am far away from here, in India or Japan, or on some more dangerous mission, I might find comfort in writing her something concerning my journeys and labors. If I should come back to this village when I am old, I, too, would like to have an intimate friendship with her, as she would be old by then, and hold spiritual chats and colloquies with her, like those the Vicar enjoys now. As I am still young, however, I seldom approach Pepita; I barely speak to her. I'd rather pass for a poltroon, a fool, a boor, and a churl than give the slightest ground, not for actually feeling toward her what I must not, but for suspicion or gossip.

I can't even remotely agree with the vague suspicion you reveal with regard to Pepita. What plan could she possibly weave around a man who is going to be a priest in two or three months? Why should she take a fancy to me when she has rebuffed so many others? I know myself and recognize that, fortunately, I cannot inspire passion. They say I'm not ugly, but I am awkward, maladroit, diffident, dull; I wear the earmarks of what I am—an humble student. Who am I compared to the handsome, though somewhat rustic, young bachelors who have paid court to Pepita—fine horsemen, discreet and gay in conversation, hunters like Nimrod, dextrous in all the bodily skills, singers famed at all the fairs in Andalusia, and dashing, elegant, and expert dancers? If Pepita has rejected all of them, how can she take a fancy now to me? How could she conceive the diabolical desire and more diabolical plan to upset my peace of mind, to make me abandon my vocation, and perhaps lose my soul? No, that isn't possible. I consider Pepita good, and, without any false modesty, I consider myself insignificant—too insignificant for her to fall in love with, but not to like as a friend; not too insignificant for her to esteem, to feel a kind of predilection for, some day when I have succeeded in making myself worthy of such liking by a devout and hard-working life.

Forgive me if I defend myself with excessive heat from certain accusations and dark forebodings I seem to read between the lines of your letter.

I am not complaining of what you have not specifically said; you are offering me prudent advice, which I accept and intend to follow. If your suspicions are a little unfair to me, that is doubtless because you take such an interest in me, and I thank you for it with all my heart.

May 4.

It seems strange that I haven't had time to write to you for so many days; but so it is. My father gives me little time to myself and I am besieged with visitors.

In big cities it is easy not to receive guests, to isolate oneself, to create a solitude, a Thebaid [10] in the midst of turmoil. In an Andalusian village, particularly when one has the honor to be the local political leader's son, one has to live in the public gaze. The Vicar, the scrivener, my cousin Currito, Doña Casilda's son, and many other people invade not merely the room where I am writing, but even my bedroom, and no one ventures to oppose them. They awaken me if I'm asleep, and I am at their beck and call.

The Casino is no mere nocturnal diversion here; it is in full swing at all hours of the day. From eleven o'clock in the morning it is full of people who chat, skim through a newspaper, and play cards. There are those who spend ten or twelve hours a day at this pastime. In short, idleness could not be more

---

[10] *A religious political entity under the sacerdotal rule in the eleventh century, founded on the ruins of the ancient necropolis of Thebes in upper Egypt.*

entertaining than here. The amusements to while away this idleness are manifold. In addition to these games of cards, including *monte*, games of chance are often going on. Checkers, chess, and dominoes are not neglected. Finally, cockfighting is a great passion.

All this is the daily business of the gentlemen, or the young gentlemen, or whatever they want to be called, together with social calls, trips to the country to inspect the farm work, checking over accounts with the overseer every night, visiting the shops and wine cellars, clarifying, decanting, and grading the wines, and haggling with the gypsies and dealers over the purchase, the sale, the bartering of horses, mules, and burros, and with the people from Jerez who come to buy our wine to use as a base for sherry. At the appropriate season, other occupations and amusements make life even more animated, as at harvest time, during the vintage, and when the olives are picked. Then there is a fair and bullfight here or in some nearby village; or a pilgrimage to the shrine of some miraculous image of the Most Blessed Virgin Mary, where, though a good many of them go out of curiosity, to amuse themselves and buy a trinket or a scapulary for their girls, more of them go out of devotion or to fulfill a vow. One of these shrines is on the top of a very high mountain, yet many and many a delicate woman still climbs it barefoot, wounding her feet on thistles, thorns, and stones along the steep, rough path.

Life here has a certain charm. I understand how it can be a very restful, sweet life for one who has no dreams of glory, no ambitious strivings. Even solitude might be achieved here, with enough effort. As I am here only for a short time, I cannot and must not make the effort; but if I were living here, I would not find it difficult to shut myself up without offending anyone, and withdraw for hours or an entire day to devote myself to my studies and meditations.

Your recent and latest letter has upset me a little. I see that you persist in your suspicions, and I don't know what to answer beyond what I have already said to justify myself.

You say that in certain types of battle, victory lies in flight; that to flee is to conquer. How can I deny what the Apostle and so many Holy Fathers and doctors of theology have said? But after all, you know very well that taking flight does not depend upon my will alone. My father does not want me to go; he keeps me here in spite of myself, and I have to obey him. So I must win by other means, but not by flight.

To set your mind at rest, I repeat that the battle has hardly been joined; that you are seeing matters as farther advanced than they actually are.

There is not the slightest indication that Pepita Jiménez cares for me. But even if she did, it would be in some way other than that of the women you cite as cautionary examples to me. In our day, a well-bred, upright woman is neither so fiery nor so bold as those ladies who fill the pages of ancient history.

The passage you quote from Saint John Chrysostom[11] is worthy of the greatest respect, but it is not altogether appropriate to the circumstances. The great lady who in Of, Thebes, or Diospolis Magna, fell in love with the favorite son of Jacob, must have been very beautiful, otherwise it is inconceivable that the saint could assure us that Joseph's failure to respond to her advances constituted a miracle greater than that of the three youths whom Nebuchadnezzar had cast into the fiery furnace and were not burned to ashes.

I am naive enough to confess that, when it comes to beauty, I cannot believe that the wife of that Egyptian prince,

---

[11] St. John Chrysostom (345-407), the greatest of the Greek Fathers of the Church. His writings stress the ascetic element in religion and the importance of knowing the Scriptures.

chief steward, or whatever he was in Pharaoh's palace, could have surpassed Pepita Jiménez. But then neither am I Joseph, a man endowed with so many gifts and parts, nor is Pepita a woman devoid of religion and decorum. But even if that were so, even envisaging such horrors, I cannot explain to myself Saint John Chrysostom's exaggerations on any basis except that he was living in the corrupt and still semi-pagan capital of the Late Empire, in that court whose vices he censured so harshly and where the Empressa Eudoxia herself set an example of corruption and scandal. But today, when the morality of the Gospel has taken deeper root in a Christian society, it seems to me an exaggeration to believe that Jacob's son's chaste rejection was more miraculous than the incombustibility of the three youths in Babylon.

In your letter you have touched on another point that greatly encourages and flatters me. You condemn, as you should, the excessive sentimentality and tendency to turn soft and weep for childish reasons which I told you comes over me at times. But even though this effeminate tendency exists in me and must be rooted out, you nevertheless praise me for not letting it become mingled with my prayers and meditations and thus contaminate them. You recognize and applaud in me the manly energy that must go hand in hand with the affections and the intelligence that yearns to lift itself to God. The mind that struggles to understand Him must be vigorous; the will that submits completely does so because it has first triumphed over itself through pitiless battles against all appetites and through conquering and putting to flight all temptations. The same purified and ardent love which, even in simple, timid creatures, can soar to God in rapture, and come to know Him through supernatural illumination, is the product of a firm, steadfast character as well as of divine grace. That languor, that breakdown of the will, that sickly tenderness has nothing to do with

charity, with devotion, and divine love. The former are attributes of an order lower than women; the latter are passions,
if passions they can be called, of a higher order than man, of
angels. Yes, you are right to have faith in me and to trust that
I shall not be ruined through a slack, soft piety, which may
open my heart to vice and come to tolerate it. God will save
me, and with His help I shall fight to save myself; but if I am
lost, it will not be because mortal sin and the enemies of the
soul have entered it in disguise, nor as a result of the surrender
of the fortress of my conscience, but only after mortal combat,
with banners flying, carrying all by fire and sword.

During these past few days I have had occasion to exercise
all the patience at my command and to mortify my self-love
in the cruelest fashion.

My father wanted to repay Pepita's garden party, and he
invited her to visit his country house in Pozo de la Solana. The
trip was set for the 22nd of April. I shall not forget that date.

Pozo de la Solana lies more than two leagues from this
village and is linked to it by bridle paths. We all had to go on
horseback. As I never learned to ride, I had accompanied my
father on all our previous excursions astride a very gentle
ambling mule, which, as the muleteer, Dientes, puts it, is
nobler than gold and easier than a carriage. I rode the same
mount on the trip to Pozo de la Solana.

My father, the notary, the druggist, and my cousin Currito
all rode good horses. My aunt, Doña Casilda, who weighs more
than two hundred and fifty pounds went side-saddle on an
enormous and powerful burro; the Vicar on a calm, gentle mule
like mine.

As for Pepita Jiménez, I had imagined that she, too, would
be riding side-saddle on a burro, for I did not know she was a
horsewoman. She surprised me by appearing in a riding habit

on a dappled horse, very lively and mettlesome, which she managed with notable skill and verve.

I was happy to see Pepita looking so dashing on horseback; but I suddenly realized the awkward figure I must cut bringing up the rear alongside Doña Casilda and the Vicar, as peaceful and calm as in a carriage, while the bright cavalcade pranced, ran, trotted, and performed a thousand feats of horsemanship. I began to feel mortified.

Immediately it occurred to me that Pepita was looking at me with compassion for the pitiful figure I must have cut astride the mule. My cousin Currito sent me a mocking smile and began to make fun of me and torment me.

Applaud my resignation and my patience. I took everything good-naturedly, and soon Currito's jokes began to fall flat before my apparent invulnerability. But how I suffered inwardly! They ran, they galloped, they dashed ahead of us, going and coming. The Vicar and I remained consistently sedate, like the mules, with no change of pace, squiring Doña Casilda between us.

I was denied even the consolation of talking with the Vicar, whose conversation is so pleasant, or of withdrawing within myself to call up fantasies and to dream, or of admiring the beauty of the countryside we were passing through. Doña Casilda is abominably loquacious, and we had to listen to her. She repeated the village gossip to the last item; she told us all about her many talents; she explained to us how to make sausages, head-cheese, puff-paste, and a thousand other dishes and delicacies. According to her, no one can surpass her in the art of cooking and meat-curing except Antonoña, the former nurse of Pepita Jiménez, and now her housekeeper and chatelaine. I had already met that Antonoña, for she goes and comes to the house on errands and is indeed very clever; as talkative as Aunt Casilda, but a thousand times more intelligent.

The road to Pozo de la Solana is delightful, but I was so out of sorts that I could not enjoy it. When we reached the outbuildings and dismounted, a great weight was lifted off me, as though I had been carrying the mule, not the mule me.

Once on foot, we walked about the property, which is magnificent, varied, and extensive. It contains more than one hundred twenty *fanegas*[12] of grape-bearing and newly-planted vineyards, all in one tract; another of olive trees on a tract as large or larger; and finally, a grove of the largest evergreen oaks still to be found in all Andalusia. The water of Pozo de le Solana forms a clear and abundant stream, where all the little birds in the vicinity come to drink and where they can be caught by the hundreds in snares of esparto grass and bird-lime, or with a net in the center of which a decoy tied to a string is placed. I was reminded of my childhood amusements and the many times I had gone to hunt birds in that way.

There are many poplars and other tall trees following the course of the stream, particularly in the ravines. Together with the shrubs and the grass, they form an intricate labyrinth and a dense thicket. A thousand sweet-scented woodland plants grow wild there, and it would be hard to imagine anything more secluded, sylvan, and truly solitary, peaceful and silent than those glades. In the heat of mid-day when the sun pours torrents of light from a cloudless sky and during the warm and restful siestas, one might experience there the same mysterious fears as in the night hours. The life of the ancient patriarchs and the primitive heroes and herdsmen may be pictured in the imagination, as well as the apparitions and visions they experienced—of nymphs, deities, and angels glimpsed in the noon-day light.

As we were walking through that thicket, there came a

---

[12] *A fanega is 1.59 acres.*

moment, I cannot say how, when Pepita and I found ourselves alone; I was at her side. The others had remained behind.

Then I felt a tremor run through all my body. That was the first time I had been alone with that woman in a place so removed, and at the very time when I was thinking of noonday apparitions, now sinister, now sweet, and always supernatural, which men used to see in ages long remote.

Pepita had left her riding skirt in the shed, and was walking in a short dress that did not hamper the graceful lightness of her movements. On her head she was wearing at a charming angle a little Andalusian hat. In her hand she carried a whip, which I fancied was a wand that that sorceress could wave to bewitch me.

I am not afraid to repeat here my eulogies of her beauty. To me she looked even more beautiful in that wild spot. The precautions ascetic men have recommended—to think of her grown ugly with age and infirmities, of imagining her dead, full of fetor and corruption, the prey of worms—came to my mind in spite of myself. I say in spite of myself, for I doubt such a dire precaution was necessary. No wrong idea, no suggestion of the evil spirit had come to overturn my reason or to corrupt my will and my senses.

What did occur to me was an argument nullifying the virtue of that precaution, at least for me. Beauty, that sovereign and divine work of art, may be weak and ephemeral, may vanish in an instant; but the idea of it is eternal, and once perceived by mortal mind, lives a life immortal. The beauty of this woman, as I behold it today, will fade within a few short years; that elegant form, those slender contours, that noble head, so gallantly poised, all will be food for loathsome worms. But even though matter must change, who can destroy the form, the artistic impulse, the beauty itself? Does it not exist in the divine mind? Once perceived and known by me, will it not live on in my soul, triumphant over age, and even over death?

I was meditating along those lines while Pepita and I were together. And those thoughts calmed my spirit and mitigated the doubts you had infused in me. I wanted, and at the same time did not want, the others to join us. I was happy, yet at the same time distressed at being alone with that woman.

Pepita's silvery voice broke the silence and roused me from my meditations as she said: "How silent and sad you are, Don Luis! It grieves me to think that perhaps through my fault, in part at least, your father has made you suffer today by bringing you to these remote regions of the country and taking you away from more remote regions of the mind where you have nothing to distract you from your prayers and your religious reading."

I don't know what I answered. I must have made some foolish reply because I was upset; but I did not want to pay Pepita a compliment, to speak worldly and gallant words, nor did I wish to answer her rudely.

She went on: "Forgive me if I am impertinent; but I imagine there is something more than your displeasure at being separated from your favorite occupations that is contributing strongly to your low spirits."

"What is the something more," I said, "since you have glimpsed, or think you have glimpsed everything?"

"That something more," Pepita replied, "is a feeling more appropriate to a young man of twenty-two than to one so soon to become a priest."

At her words I felt the blood rise to my face and set my cheeks afire. A thousand wild ideas flocked into my mind; I fancied I was prey to an obsession. I decided that Pepita was provoking me, that she was about to let me know that she was aware of my liking for her. Then my timidity turned to bold arrogance, and I looked her straight in the eye. My stare must have seemed slightly ridiculous, but either Pepita did not notice it, or she concealed her awareness beneath a kindly prudence, saying with an air of great simplicity: "Don't be offended with me for pointing out a fault, one I've noticed and that seems to me very slight. You're hurt by Currito's jokes and by playing a sorry role, to put it bluntly, jogging along on a gentle mule, like the Vicar with his eighty years, instead of riding a spirited horse, as a young man of your age and circumstances should. That is the fault of the Dean, for he hasn't taken into consideration that you ought to know how to ride. Horsemanship can fit well into the life you intend to follow, and I think that now you're here, your father ought to be able to teach you in a few days. If you should go to Persia or China, you wouldn't find any railroads, and you'd cut a poor figure if you rode badly. Your mission among the barbarians might suffer through such a lack of skill, and that would make it harder for you to reap the fruit of your preachings."

Pepita marshalled these and other reasons why I should learn to ride horseback, and I became so convinced that horsemanship would be useful to a missionary that I promised her I would ask my father to teach me immediately.

"The next time we go on an outing," I said, "I will be astride my father's most mettlesome horse instead of the ambling mule I'm on today."

"I shall be very glad," Pepita answered with a smile of inexpressible sweetness.

Just then all the others arrived at the place where we were. Inwardly I was glad, for no reason other than that I was afraid I might be incapable of holding up my end of the conversation and would come out with a couple of hundred commonplaces, for I have had little or no practice in talking with women.

After our walk, my father's servants set out an abundant

picnic lunch on the cool grass beside the stream, in the loveliest spot. The conversation was animated and Pepita displayed a nice wit and discretion. My cousin Currito again started to ridicule my style of riding and the gentleness of my mule. He called me a theologian, adding that I looked as though I were scattering blessings as I rode along on muleback. This time I countered his jokes with a wit that came easily owing to my firm resolve to become a horseman. I said nothing about my previous commitment to learn to ride, however. Pepita doubtless thought, like me, that it was important to keep it secret so that I could surprise him later with my skill, and although there had been no word of agreement between us, she did not mention our conversation. Thus it came about simply and naturally that we had a secret between us, and this produced a curious effect on my mind.

Nothing else worthy of the telling happened that day.

In the afternoon we went back to the village as we had come. But on the return trip I was not bored and low-spirited on my docile mule alongside Aunt Casilda, as I had been while going. All along the way I could hear my aunt tirelessly telling her stories, but for whole minutes I was lost in vague imaginings.

Nothing that takes place in my soul should be kept from you. I must tell you that Pepita's image was the center, or better, the nucleus and focus of my vagrant fancies.

The vision of her in the full light of noonday in the greenest, leafiest, shadiest, and most silent part of the wildwood brought to my memory all the good and evil apparitions of portentous beings from a plane higher than ours, that I had read about in the classic works of religious and secular authors. Pepita took shape before my eyes and on the stage of my inner fantasies, not as she was moving along on horseback ahead of us, but in an ideal and ethereal manner, as his mother appeared

to Aeneas[13] in the seclusion of a forest, as Pallas[14] to Calimachus, as the sylph who later conceived Dibusa appeared to
the Bohemian shepherd Kroko,[15] as Diana to the son of Ari-
steus,[16] as the angels in the valley of Mambré to the Patriarch,
as the centaur to Saint Anthony[17] in the solitude of the desert.

I find it natural that the ideal of Pepita became transformed in my mind into something of a marvel. For a moment
when I realized the consistency of this vision, I thought I was
obsessed. Nothing had occurred during the few minutes I was
alone with Pepita near the stream at La Solana, nothing in fact
that was not natural and commonplace. But I fancied, as I was
going along peaceably on my mule, that some demon was in-
visibly at work around me, suggesting a thousand absurdities.

That night I told my father I wanted to learn to ride. I
did not try to conceal from him that Pepita had urged me to it.
Father was extraordinarily pleased. He embraced me, he kissed
me, he said you were no longer my only teacher. Now he, too,
was going to have the pleasure of teaching me something.
Finally he assured me that within two or three weeks, he would
make me the best horseman in all Andalusia, a rider capable
of going to Gibraltar for contraband and returning with a bag
of tobacco and a load of smuggled cotton and show the customs
officers a clean pair of heels. In short, I'd be able to strike awe

---

[13] *Hero of* The Aeneid, *the Latin epic poem by Vergil, glorifying
the founding of Rome, and the wanderings of Aeneas after the fall of
Troy.*

[14] *Pallas Athena, goddess of wisdom, appeared to the sculptor
Calimachus, who was inspired to invent the running drill for making
folds in drapery in sculpture and the Corinthian capital.*

[15] *Probably Crocus, the shepherd who loved the nymph, Smilax.*

[16] *Actaeon, who saw Diana bathing and was punished for his daring
by being turned into a stag that was killed by his own hounds.*

[17] *One of St. Anthony's temptations in the desert. In his oft-repeated
struggles with the hosts of evil, the saint was often beaten and left
for dead. Many of his antagonists were mythical beasts, such as the
Centaur.*

into the best horsemen at the fairs in Seville and Mairena. I'd
be ready to dig my heels into the flanks of Babieca,[18] Buce-
phalus,[19] even the horses of the sun,[20] if by any chance they
should descend to earth so that I could seize them by the bridle.

I don't know what you are going to think of my learning
this art of equitation; but I presume you will take it in good
part.

If you could see how pleased my father is and how he
delights in teaching me! Since the day after the outing I've already told you about, I have been taking two lessons a day.
Some days the lesson is continuous because we spend it on
horseback. The first week the lessons were held in the unpaved
stable-yard, which served us as a riding ring.

Now we are going out to the fields, trying not to let anyone see us. Father wants me not to show myself in public until,
he says, I can astonish everyone with my good seat. Unless his
paternal vanity is deceiving him, this should be very soon, for
I have the natural qualifications to be a good rider.

"It's plain to see that you're my son!" Father exclaims
jubilantly as he watches my progress.

Father is such a good man that I hope you will forgive
him his profane language and his irreverent jests. I tolerate all
such things, though my heart grieves within me.

I have the most painful saddle sores from the long, uninter-
rupted lessons. Father tells me to write you that I am mortifying
the flesh this way. He assures me he will graduate me, but he
is most reluctant to resign his position as a teacher. Consequently, he suggests other studies, time-wasting and ill suited
to a future priest. One day he wants to teach me how to over-

---

[18] *The Cid's war horse.*
[19] *Alexander the Great's horse.*
[20] *Phaethon, son of Helios, who drove his chariot too close to the
earth.*

turn a bull so that he can take me to Seville and give the bully boys and iron men an eye-opener, with pike in hand on the plains at Tablada. Another day he recalls his younger days as a guardsman and says he's going to look for his foils, gloves, and masks in order to teach me fencing. And finally, as he fancies he can use a knife better than anybody, he has even offered to teach me that skill, too.

You can readily imagine how I reply to such nonsense. But Father retorts that in the good old days, even the bishops, to say nothing of the clergy, used to ride around on horseback, running infidels through. I mention to him that such things might have happened in barbarous times, but that now the ministers of the All Highest need have recourse to no other arms than persuasion.

"And when persuasion it not enough," adds Father, "isn't it a good thing to back up an argument with a few blows?"

As my father sees things, the fully equipped missionary must resort on occasion to such heroic means, and harking back to the many novels and romances he has read, he will cite examples to support his opinion. He gives first place to Saint James who cut down more Moors with the sword while he was still an apostle, than he persuaded and preached to from his white horse. He cites the Señor de la Vera[21] whom the Catholic Sovereigns sent as an emissary to Boabdil, the last of the Moorish kings, and who in the Court of the Lions in the Alhambra, involved the Moors in theological disputation, until weary of reasoning with them, he drew his sword and charged them, determined to convert them by main force. Finally Father cites the Basque hidalgo, Don Iñigo de Loyola[22] and points out

---

[21] *Pedro de la Vera, Hidalgo de Jerez de la Frontera, who carried out several military and judicial commissions for Ferdinand and Isabel.*

[22] *Saint Ignatius of Loyola. In his youth he was a soldier, later a militant priest who in 1539 founded the Company of Jesus, which is ruled by military discipline.*

that in the course of a controversy with a Moor over the purity
of the Most Blessed Virgin Mary, he grew so angry at the
impious and horrifying blasphemies with which the Moor contradicted him that he fell upon the infidel sword in hand, and
if the Moor had not taken to his heels, he would have carried
conviction to his soul by desperate means. While we were dis-
cussing St. Ignatius, I told Father that all that happened before the saint became a priest and added that the other examples were not germane.

In short, I defend myself from Father's jokes as best I can,
limiting myself to learning to be a good horseman without
studying those other activities, so inappropriate to priests,
though Father assures me that not a few Spanish priests are
versed in such skills and frequently exercise them in Spain
even today for the triumph of the faith and conservation or
restoration of Catholic unity.

It weighs upon my heart that Father is like this. He speaks
irreverently and jokingly of the most serious matters. But it
would be unseemly for a respectful son to go beyond the point
to which I go in repressing his somewhat Voltairean outbursts.
I call them Voltairean because I don't know just what else to
call them. At heart Father is a good Catholic and this comforts
me.

Yesterday was the Day of the Cross, and the village was
very animated. In every street six or seven May crosses were
set up and covered with flowers, but none was as beautiful as
the one Pepita placed at the door of her house. Her cross was
a mass of flowers.

In the evening we went to a party at Pepita's house. The
cross that had been in the street was set up in a large parlor on
the main floor where she has a piano and where she prepared
for us a simple, poetic tableau, which I had seen done as a
child, though I had not remembered it.

From the head of the cross hung seven ribbons or streamers—two white, two green, and three red, the colors symbolizing the seven Sacraments. Seven little boys of five or six who represented the seven Sacraments, held the seven ribbons hanging from the cross. They performed a kind of *contredanse* that was very well done. Baptism was a child dressed as a catechumen in his white tunic; Holy Orders, another little boy as a priest; Confirmation, a little bishop; Extreme Unction, a pilgrim with a staff and a shell-trimmed cloak; Matrimony, two sweethearts; and Penance, a Nazarene with a cross and a crown of thorns.

Rather than an actual dance, the *contredanse* was a series of bows, steps, turns, and genuflexions in time to fairly good music, something like a march, which the organist played on the piano with considerable skill.

After they had played their parts, the little boys, children of servants and friends in Pepita's house, went to bed loaded down with gifts and goodies.

The party went on until midnight. Refreshments were served: little cups of preserved fruit, and finally chocolate with cakes and sugar water.

Since spring arrived Pepita's retirement and solitude have been laid aside, to my father's gratification. Henceforth, Pepita will be at home to guests every night, and Father wants me to be a member of the group.

Pepita has put off her mourning and looks more colorful and gay, though always modest, in light, almost summery dresses.

I am hoping that my father will keep me here no longer than the remainder of this month. In June we shall go together to the city, and you will see then how happy I shall be to embrace you and to attain my goal of becoming a priest, free of Pepita, who will never think of me again nor remember me for good or ill.

May 7.

Every night from nine to twelve we gather at Pepita's house, as I have already told you. There are four or five ladies, including my Aunt Casilda, an equal number of unmarried girls from the village, and six or seven young gentlemen who generally play games of forfeits with the young girls. Naturally, there are three or four engaged couples.

The more sedate group is always the same. You might say it is made up of the high officials: my father, who is the political leader, the druggist, the doctor, the notary, and the Vicar.

Pepita plays cards with my father, the Vicar, and some other guests.

I don't know where I belong. If I join the young people, I disturb their games and flirtations with my seriousness. If I go with my elders, I have to play the role of a mere watcher of something I don't understand. The only card game I know is "blind donkey" and "seeing donkey," plus a little bit about *tute* or *brisca*.

It would be best for me not to go to the gathering; but Father insists upon it. According to him, I'd look ridiculous if I didn't go.

Whenever Father becomes aware of my ignorance of certain things, he is amazed. For instance, he is astounded at my not knowing how to play cards, not even *tresillo*.

He keeps saying to me, "Your uncle has brought you up under a bell glass, poking theology and more theology down your throat, and leaving you in darkness about everything else there is to know. As you're planning to be a priest, and won't be able to dance or play the lover at parties, obviously you need to know how to play cards, otherwise, what will you do, poor fellow?"

I have had to yield before these and similar arguments, and now Father is teaching me *tresillo* at home, so that once I know it I can play at Pepita's gatherings. I have already told you that he also wants to teach me fencing, and later to smoke, to shoot a pistol, and to throw the bar; but I have not consented to any of those plans.

"What a difference between your youth and mine!" Father exclaims. Then he adds, laughing, "But it all comes to the same thing in the end. I, too, spent my canonical hours in the barracks of the Guardsmen; my incense was a cigar, my hymn book a deck of cards, and I never lacked for other more or less spiritual devotions and exercises."

Although you had forewarned me of those habits of Father's, and although, because of them, I have spent twelve years with you, from the age of ten to twenty-two, I still become confused and upset at times by Father's often overly-free remarks. But what can we do about it? I cannot rebuke him for them, but neither do I applaud or laugh at them.

The odd and praiseworthy thing is that my father is another man when he is in Pepita's house. Never, even by chance, does a single phrase, a single joke of the sort he indulges in so freely in other places escape him there. In Pepita's house, he is circumspection personified. Moreover, he seems more smitten with her every day, with higher hopes of winning her.

Father continues to be pleased beyond words with me as a riding pupil. He assures me that in four or five more days, I shall be able to mount and ride the black horse, Lucifer, out of a mare of the Guadalcazar strain by an Arabian sire, a jumper, fleet as the wind, and full of fire and every imaginable trick.

"Anyone who can throw a leg over Lucifer can compete with the Centaurs themselves," Father says, "and you're going to be straddling him very soon."

Although I spend my entire day in the fields on horse-back, or else in the club and at social gatherings, I lie awake for hours at night, sometimes voluntarily, sometimes because sleep eludes me, and meditate on my situation and examine my conscience. Pepita's image is ever present in my soul. I ask myself, can this be love?

My moral commitment, my promise to consecrate myself to the altar, though not yet confirmed, is to me valid and all-encompassing. If something opposed to the fulfillment of that promise has entered my soul, it must be combatted.

To be sure I am aware (and don't accuse me of a pride because I say so) that my will, which you have taught me to exercise, is omnipotent over all my senses. While Moses was speaking with God on Mt. Sinai, the people below on the plain were rebelliously worshipping the golden calf. In spite of my youth my spirit has no fear of such rebellions. I could talk with God in full confidence, if the enemy did not come to contend with me in the sanctuary itself. Pepita's image appears to me in my soul. Her spirit wars against my spirit; it is the idea of her beauty in all its disembodied purity that arises before me on the road leading to the deeps of the soul where God dwells, and prevents me from reaching it.

Yet withal, I am not blind. I can see clearly; I can distinguish; I am not deceived. Above and beyond this spiritual inclination that draws me to Pepita, lies the love for the infinite and the eternal. Even though Pepita may appear before me as an idea, a poem, she never ceases to be the idea, the poem of something finite, limited, concrete, whereas the love of God and the concept of God are all-embracing. But try as I may, I cannot succeed in clothing this supreme concept, the

object of my highest devotion, in an imaginable form in order
to enable it to do battle with the image, with the memory of
the frail and ephemeral reality, that haunts me constantly. I
devoutly pray heaven to arouse and fortify my imagination so
as to create a likeness, a symbol of the concept that comprises
everything, and thus absorb and blot out the image, the memory
of this woman. It is vague, it is dark, indescribable, it is like a
deep shadow, this supreme concept and object of my love;
whereas she appears to me with definite outlines, clear luminous, plain as the light of day, with the veiled light which the
eyes of the spirit repel, but lacking that other, intense lumi-
nosity that is like shadows to the eyes of the spirit.

All other considerations, all other forms, fail to obscure
the image of this woman. It interposes itself between the
Crucifix and me; between the most devout image of the Virgin
and me; between the pages of the spiritual book I am reading
and me.

I do not believe, however, that I have been infected with
what this century calls love. And even though I were, I would
still fight and conquer it.

The daily sight of that woman, and the constant sound
of her praises being sung, even by the Vicar, all keep distracting me, turning my mind toward worldly things, and enticing
it from its proper concentration on things spiritual. But no, I
don't love Pepita yet. I will go away and forget her.

As long as I am here, I shall fight valiantly. I shall wrestle
with God until I subdue Him through love and submission.
My pleas shall fly to Him like flaming arrows, and shall destroy
the shield with which He covers Himself and hides Himself
from the eyes of my soul. I shall struggle like Israel, in the
silence of the night, and God shall wound me in the thigh and
defeat me in this contest, so that I, the vanquished, shall be the
victor.

May 12.

Dear Uncle, Father decided I should mount Lucifer sooner than I had thought. Yesterday, at six o'clock in the morning, I rode out to the country on this beautiful wild animal, as Father calls him. Father was with me, on a sorrel pony.

I did so well, and I had such a good, secure seat on that superb animal, that Father could not resist the temptation to show off his pupil. After we had rested at one of his farms, half a league from here, he had me return to the village around eleven o'clock and enter through the crowded center, dashing down the streets, and creating a great stir. Needless to say, we passed through the street where Pepita lives. For some time now she has taken to sitting at the window, and there she was, behind the grille of one that faced the street, and shaded by a green jalousie.

At the sound of the clatter we made, she looked up to see us and instantly rose, abandoned the sewing in her hands, and came to watch us. As I later learned, Lucifer had long made it a habit to show off as he passed Pepita's house. Now he began to curvet and to struggle against my hands. I tried to calm him but as both the hands and the rider were strange to him, and perhaps unworthy of his respect, he curvetted more and more and began to snort, to wheel, and even to buck a little. But I kept calm and held him with a firm hand, and to show him who was master, I rowelled him, touched him on the chest with the whip, and held him in with a tight rein. Lucifer, who had almost stood on his hind legs, then gave in, even bending his knees and making a bow.

The crowd of onlookers who had gathered around us, broke into loud applause. My father said, "Hurrah for the brave, spirited boys!"

Then noticing that Currito, who never has anything to do but walk the streets, was among the crowd, Father spoke to him directly: "Look, you knave; look at the theologian now. Instead of making fun you can stand stiff with astonishment."

Indeed Currito's mouth was hanging open; he was paralyzed, genuinely astounded.

My triumph was great and solemn, though out of keeping with my character. The unsuitability of this triumph filled me with embarrassment. My cheeks burned. I must have blushed like a pomegranate, and turned even redder when I noticed that Pepita was applauding and saluting me affectionately, with a smile and a wave of her pretty hands.

In short, I have won my spurs as a strong man and a first class horseman.

Father could not be more gratified and proud. He keeps assuring me that my education is complete now, and that though you sent him a learned book in me, it was only a rough, unbound draft that he is now finishing and binding.

Card-playing, if it is part of the finishing and binding, has also been mastered now. The last two nights I've played with Pepita.

The night following my equestrian feat, Pepita received me with enthusiasm, and did then what she had never wanted nor ventured to do with me before—she offered me her hand.

Don't think I forgot what so many, many of the moralists and ascetics recommend. Yet in my own mind, I believed they had exaggerated the danger. If the Holy Ghost holds that he who touches a woman exposes himself as though to the bite of a scorpion, it seemed to me to have some other meaning. Doubtless certain phrases and sentences of the Scriptures are interpreted very stringently in the religious books, with the most salutary intent. Otherwise, how can one understand that the beauty of a woman, such a perfect work of God, is always the cause of perdition? Or how comprehend that, always and without exception, woman is more bitter than death? How understand that he who touches a woman, on any occasion and with whatever thought in mind, will not emerge uncontaminated?

In brief, I made a rapid mental review of all such warnings, then took the hand Pepita held out to me with affection, and pressed it in my own. The softness of her hand made me more deeply conscious of its delicacy and beauty, which until then I had known only through my eyes.

According to the customs now in vogue, once the hand has been given, it must always be offered on arrival and leavetaking. I hope you will see nothing wrong or dangerous in this ceremony, this pledge of friendship, this manifestation of affection, as long as it is carried out with purity and without the slightest trace of frivolity.

As there are many evenings when Father has to be with his overseer and other people from the country until ten thirty or eleven o'clock, I have been taking his place beside Pepita at the card table. The Vicar and the notary almost always play the other hands. We gamble for a tenth of a *real,* so that a dollar or two is the most that is ever risked on the game.

We take so little interest in the game that we interrupt it constantly with pleasant conversation and even arguments over the fine points. Pepita always reveals such clarity of mind, vividness of imagination and extraordinary wit in her phrasing that I can only marvel at her.

I cannot find sufficient reason to change my opinion with regard to what I have already told you in reply to your suspicion that Pepita may feel a certain inclination toward me. She treats me with the natural affection she is bound to feel toward the son of her suitor, Don Pedro de Vargas, and with the shyness and discretion that a man in my circumstances— not yet a priest but soon to be one—should inspire.

As I always write to you as if on my knees in the confessional before you, I must tell you, indeed I want to tell you, about a quick impression I have caught two or three times; an hallucination or a moment of delirium, perhaps, yet something I have observed.

In other letters, I have mentioned that Pepita's eyes, green as Circe's, hold an expression of open candor and serenity. She might be said to be unaware of the power of her eyes, ignorant that they serve any purpose other than merely seeing. When she fixes her gaze on anyone, the sweet light of her glance is so clear, frank, and pure that far from giving rise to any evil thought, it seems to engender clean thoughts, to let innocent and chaste souls rest in peace, and to demolish and destroy any incentive in those which are not. No burning passion, no fire lies in Pepita's eyes. The ray of her glance is like the cool light of the moon.

Yet in spite of this, once or twice I seem to have glimpsed a momentary flash like lighting, a fleeting and consuming flame in those eyes as they rested on me. Can this be a ridiculous vanity suggested by the devil himself?

It seems to me it is; I want to think so, and I do.

The impression was rapid, so fleeting that I am led to conjecture that it had no extrinsic reality, that it was only a dream of mine.

What I have always found in Pepita's eyes is a heavenly calm, the coolness of personal indifference, tempered by the sweetness of friendship and charity.

Nevertheless, this daydream, this hallucination of that strange and ardent glance torments me.

Father says that women, not men, are the ones who seize the initiative, that they do so without assuming any responsibility, with the privilege of denying, and making an about face whenever they wish. According to Father, the woman is the one who declares herself through the medium of fleeting glances, whose import she later denies to her own conscience, if need be, while the man to whom such glances are directed is left to guess their meaning, rather than to read them. He who is loved can perceive, then, that he is loved by means of a kind of electric shock, a very subtle and almost indefinable intuition. And when he makes up his mind to speak, he is on firm ground and fully confident that the feeling is mutual.

Who knows whether these theories of Father's, which I listen to because I cannot help hearing them, are what has stirred me up and led me to imagine something that does not exist?

Nevertheless, I sometimes ask myself if it would be so absurd, so impossible if it were true? And if it were, if Pepita thought of me as something more than a friend, if the woman whom my father is courting should fall in love with me, wouldn't my situation be appalling? Let us cast aside these fears conjured up, no doubt by vanity. Let us not make a Phaedra[23] out of Pepita, nor a Hippolytus out of me.

What is beginning to surprise me is Father's carelessness and his complete self-confidence. Forgive me, ask God to forgive me my pride, but at times his self-confidence pricks and angers me. Am I then so ridiculous, I say to myself, that in spite of, or because of my supposed saintliness, my father has no fear that I may not win Pepita's love against my will?

I pursue a curious process of reasoning whereby I explain to myself my parent's carelessness in this important matter without wounding my self esteem. Unwarrantedly, Father must already be looking upon himself as Pepita's husband, and beginning to suffer that fatal blindness which Asmodeus or some more infamous demon instills in husbands. Profane and ecclesiastical history is full of instances of such blindness, which God doubtless permits for His own ends. Perhaps the most

---

[23] *Phaedra, the young second wife of Theseus, fell in love with her step-son, Hippolytus, and when she was repulsed, she caused him to be put to death.*

agregious example is that of the Emperor Marcus Aurelius who had a wife as lewd and vicious as Faustina, and in spite of being a man so wise and such an astute philosopher, never became aware of what was common knowledge to everyone in the Roman Empire. Consequently he gives infinite thanks to the immortal gods in the meditations and memoirs he wrote about himself, because they had granted him such a good and faithful wife, thereby making himself the laughing-stock of his contemporaries and of future generations. Since then it is a common sight to see wealthy and prominent men who appoint as their secretaries and heap their favors upon those who enjoy their wife's. In this way I can understand why Father is careless and does not suspect he might have a rival in me, even against my will.

It would show a lack of respect, and I would be guilty of presumption and insolence, if I were to warn Father of the danger to which he is blind. There is no way that I can say anything to him. In any case, what could I say? That I imagine that Pepita has looked at me once or twice in a different way than she usually does? May this not be an illusion of mine? No, I haven't the slightest proof that Pepita even wants to flirt with me.

So what could I say to Father? Am I to tell him I am the one who is in love with Pepita, that I covet the treasure he already considers his? That is not true, and even if it were, to my shame and sorrow, how could I say so to my father?

My best course is to hold my tongue; to fight in silence if temptation should actually assail me, and to try to leave this village and go back to you as soon as possible.

May 19.

Thanks be to God and to you for the new letters and new advice you have sent me. More than ever I need them today.

The mystic doctor, Saint Teresa, was right to stress the travail of weak souls who let themselves be swayed by temptation; but a thousand times more grievous is the disenchantment of those who, like me, have been self-confident and proud.

Our bodies are the temples of the Holy Ghost, but if their walls are attacked by fire, even if they do not burn, they will be smirched by soot.

The first temptation is like the serpent's head. If we do not trample it down with firm, courageous foot, the poisonous reptile will rise to seek a hiding place in our bosom.

The savor of worldly delights, however innocent, is sweet on the tongue, but later it is transformed into the gall of dragons and the venom of asps.

It is true; I can no longer deny it to you. I should not have let my eyes look with such pleasure upon this dangerous woman.

As pants the hart for cooling springs, so doth my soul still seek God, turn to Him for repose, seek refreshment at His hands in the torrent whose flood delights all Paradise, whose clear stream makes all purer than the driven snow; but deep calls to deep, and my feet have sunk deep in the mire of the abyss.

Yet I still have voice and breath to cry out with the Psalmist: "Arise, O Lord; let not man prevail." "They shall not prevail against thee, for I am with thee . . ."

I say to my sinful soul, so filled with chimerical imaginings and the vague desires which are their bastard offspring: O, wretched daughter of Babylon, blessed is he who will give thee thy just deserts; blessed is he who will dash thy children against the stones.

Mortifications, fasting, prayer, penance, will be the weapons with which I shall arm myself to fight and conquer, with divine aid.

It was not a dream; it was not madness; it was a fact. She looks at me at times with the burning gaze I have already mentioned to you. Her eyes are endowed with an inexplicable and magnetic attraction. She draws me to her, seduces me, and my eyes become fixed on hers. At such times my eyes must burn like hers with an unholy light; like those of Amon when he looked upon Tamar;[24] like those of the Prince of Siquem when he looked upon Dinah.[25]

When we look at each other like that, I forget even God. Her image rises from the depths of my spirit, triumphant over all else. Her beauty shines above all beauty; the delights of heaven seem to me less than her love; I think an eternity of suffering would not be too much to pay for the infinite blessedness she sheds on me in a moment with one of those glances that come and go like lightning.

When I am at home again, alone in my room in the silence of the night, I recognize to the full the horror of my situation, and I make good resolutions that are later broken.

I promise myself I will feign illness, seek any pretext whatsoever so as not to go to Pepita's house the next night, and yet I go.

Supremely trusting, never suspecting what is going on in my soul, my father says to me when the hour comes, "Go to the gathering. I'll come later, after I've finished with the overseer."

I search in vain for an excuse; I can't find a pretext, and instead of saying, "I'd rather not go," I pick up my hat and leave.

As I enter Pepita and I shake hands, and at her touch, I

---

[24] *Tamar, daughter of King David and the victim of her half-brother Amon's passion.*

[25] *Dinah was the daughter of Jacob and Leah. Shechem, son of Hamor, son of the Hivite chieftain, violated her.*

am bewitched. My whole being is transformed. A devouring fire enters my heart, and I can think of nothing but her. Perhaps I myself call forth her glances, if they are slow to come. Irresistibly aroused, I look at her with a mad longing, and think every moment I seem to find new perfections in her: now the dimples in her cheeks when she smiles, now the rosy whiteness of her skin, now the straight line of her nose, now the smallness of her ear, now the smooth contours and wonderfully molded lines of her throat.

In spite of myself I go into her house as though summoned by sorcery; and no sooner am I there than I fall under her spell. I see clearly that I am in the toils of a sorceress whose fascination is inescapable.

Nor is she pleasing only to my eyes; her words ring in my ears like the music of the spheres, revealing to me all the harmony of the universe, and I fancy I can sense a most subtle fragrance given off by her immaculate body, surpassing the scent of mint that thrives by the banks of streams and the aroma of wild thyme that grows on the slopes of hills.

In this state of the mind, I do not know how I play cards or talk or reason, for I am completely absorbed in her.

Each time our glances meet, our souls go with them, and each time the rays from our eyes cross, they meet and merge. A thousand ineffable mysteries of love are disclosed, feelings that would otherwise remain hidden are thus communicated, poetry wells up that tongue cannot compass, and songs sung that no voice can express nor well-tempered zither attune.

Since that day at Pozo de la Solana, I have never seen Pepita alone. I have said nothing to her nor she to me, and yet we have told each other everything.

Alone at night in my room, withdrawn from her fascination, I cast a cold eye upon the state I am in, I see the chasm yawning before me, and I feel that I am slipping and falling.

You urge me to think about death; not the death of this woman but my own. You recommend that I think of the instability, the insecurity of our life and of what lies beyond. But such considerations and meditations neither frighten nor deter me. How can I fear death when I want to die? Love and death are brothers. A feeling of renunciation rises from the depths of my being, and calls to me, telling me that I must yield all of my self to the beloved object and be lost. What I long for is to lose myself in one of her glances; melt away and evaporate in the ray of light that shines from her eyes, to die gazing on her, even though I be damned for it.

To me the counterbalance to love is not fear, but love itself. Above and beyond this finite love which I clearly see that Pepita inspires in me, divine love arises in my spirit in a potent revivification. Everything in me is transformed then, and I promise myself that victory will still be mine. The object of my higher love appears before my mind's eye like the sun that glows and illuminates, filling all space with light, while the object of my baser love is like a dust mote that dances in the air and is gilded by the sun. All her beauty, all her splendor, all her attractions are mere reflections of that divine sun, nothing but the brilliant, transitory, mutable spark from that infinite and eternal flame.

My soul glows with love, struggles to acquire wings, to take flight and mount to that blaze where all its impurities will be consumed.

For several days now my life has been a constant struggle. I don't know why the malady from which I suffer does not show itself on my face. I can scarcely eat, scarcely sleep. If my weary eyes close, I wake up with a start, as though I were engaged in a battle between the good and the rebellious angels. In this struggle between light and darkness, I am fighting on the side of light; but perhaps I imagine that I shall go over to the enemy, become a base deserter, and I can hear the voice of the eagle of Patmos[26] saying: "And men prefer darkness to light." Then terror fills me, and I give myself up for lost.

I have no choice but to flee. If Father does not give me leave to go by the end of the month, and does not come with me, I shall run away like a thief. I shall flee without a word.

May 23.

I am a vile worm, not a man; I am the shame and the disgrace of humanity; I am a hypocrite.

I am encircled by the pangs of death, and am tossed in the flood waters of iniquity.

I am ashamed to write to you, yet I am writing. I want to confess everything.

I have not succeeded in mending my ways. Far from ceasing to go to Pepita's house, I go earlier every night. One would say that demons take me by the feet and drag me there against my will.

Fortunately, I never find Pepita alone. I should not want to find her alone. The excellent Vicar is almost always there before me. He attributes our friendship to a similarity of pious tastes, based on devotion, like the wholly innocent friendship he feels for her.

The progress of my malady has been swift. My soul is now like a stone falling from the top of a church, gaining speed as it falls.

When Pepita and I shake hands, it is no longer as it was in the beginning. We voluntarily transmit to each other the beating of our hearts through our joined right hands. It seems

---

[26] *St. John the Evangelist, who is said to have written the* Apocalypse *in a high mountain retreat near Patmos.*

as though we work a transfusion by some devilish art, mingling the subtlest components of our blood. She must feel my life circulate through her veins as I feel hers in mine.

When I am near her, I love her; when I am away from her, I hate her. I fall in love at the sight of her; in her presence I am attracted to her; she gently conquers me, she lowers over my neck the sweetest of yokes.

The memory of her is killing me. When I dream of her, I dream she is cutting my throat as did Judith[27] the Assyrian captain's, or that she is driving a nail into my temple, as Jael pierced Sisera's.[28] But when she is beside me, she seems the spouse in the Song of Songs, and I call her with an inner voice, and bless her, and I think she is a fountain sealed up, a garden enclosed, a flower of the valley, a lily of the fields, my dove, and my sister.

I want to free myself of this woman and I cannot. I abhor her, yet I adore her. Her spirit enters into me to the point that I see her before my eyes; she possesses me, she dominates me, and she humbles me.

Each night I leave her house saying, "This will be the last night I come here," and the next night I go back.

When she speaks, and I am at her side, my soul hangs upon her words; when she smiles, it is as if a ray of celestial light had entered my heart and gladdened it.

At times as we were playing cards, our knees have accidentally touched and I have felt an indescribable thrill.

---

[27] *When the Jews were attacked by an army under Holofernes, Judith, a beautiful widow, approached him, won his favor, murdered him, and returned to show his head to the Israelites.*

[28] *Sisera was the leader of the Canaanite army, which attacked the Israelites and was routed. Sisera fled on foot to the tent of the wife of Heber the Kenite, Jael, who killed him while he was asleep by driving a tentpin into his temple.*

Take me away from here. Write to my father to give me leave to go. Tell him everything, if you must. Help me! Be my refuge!

May 30.

God has given me the strength to resist, and I have resisted.

For several days now, I have not set foot in Pepita's house nor have I seen her.

I scarcely need to pretend an illness, for I am really ill. I am pale and hollow-eyed. Father is all affectionate solicitude. He keeps asking me what is the matter and showing the greatest interest in me.

The kingdom of heaven can be stormed, and I long to invest it. I cry at its gates with a mighty voice, asking that they be opened to me.

God is feeding me on wormwood to try me, and I beg Him in vain to let this cup of bitterness pass from me; but I have been spending and still spend many wakeful nights in prayer, and an inspiration from the comforting and sovereign spirit has come to sweeten the bitterness of the chalice.

I have beheld the promised land with the eyes of my soul, and the new song of the heavenly Jerusalem has resounded in the depths of my heart.

If in the end I triumph, the victory will be a glorious one; but I shall owe it to the Queen of the Angels, to whom I have commended myself. She is my refuge and my shield; my Tower of David, hung with a thousand swords and the armor of valiant warriors; the Cedar of Lebanon, who puts the serpent to flight.

On the other hand, I am trying to abase and pluck from my thoughts the woman who has enamored me, reminding myself of the words of the Wise Man and applying them to her:

Thou art snare of the hunter, I say to her; thy heart is a net of deceit, and thy hands are cords that bind; he who loves God will flee from thee, but the sinner will become thy prisoner.

Meditating on love, I find a thousand reasons for loving God and not loving her.

In the depths of my heart I feel an ineffable strength that convinces me I shall despise everything for the love of God: fame, honor, power, and empire. I find myself capable of imitating Christ; and if the tempter should lead me to the top of a mountain and there offer me all the kingdoms of earth if I but bowed before him, I would not bend my knee. But when he offers me this woman, I still hesitate and I do not refuse him. Is this woman worth more in my eyes than all the kingdoms of earth? More than fame, honor, power, and empire?

Sometimes I ask myself whether the virtue of love remains the same however diverse the objects to which it is given, or whether there are two types and manners of love. To love God seems to me the denial of selfishness and exclusiveness. Loving Him, I can and would love all things through Him, and I am not angered nor envious because He loves all things. I am not jealous nor envious of the saints, the martyrs, the blessed, nor the very seraphim. And the more I consider the love of God for His creatures and how He smiles upon them, and the gifts He gives them, the less jealous I am and the more I love Him; the nearer He seems to me, and the more loving and kind to me. My brotherhood—my more than brotherhood—with all living creatures springs up anew then, in a fashion most sweet. It seems to me that I am one with everything, and that everything is bound together in God and in the bonds of God's love.

But when I think of this woman and the love she inspires in me—a love-hate that draws me away from everything but myself—I see everything in reverse. I love her for myself, all to myself, and I want to be all to her. Even my devotion to her and my sacrifice for her would be selfish. To die for her would mean that I despaired of winning her through other means, or hoped to be able to enjoy her love completely only by dying and being linked to her in an eternal embrace.

Through such thoughts, I am trying to make the love of this woman abhorrent. I ascribe to this love much that is infernal and horribly ominous; but as though I had two souls, two minds, two wills, and two imaginations, the opposite quickly occurs to me. I promptly deny to myself what I have just affirmed, and try madly to reconcile my two loves. Why do I not flee from her, while loving her still, even as I dedicate myself fervently to the service of God? Just as the love of God does not exclude the love of country, the love for humanity, the love of learning, the love of beauty in nature and art, it should not exclude this love either, if it is spiritual and immaculate. I tell myself I shall make of her a symbol, an allegory, an image of all that is good and beautiful. She will be to me as Beatrice[29] to Dante, the embodiment and image of my country, of wisdom and of beauty.

This plunges me, however, into a monstrous thought, a hideous vision. To make of Pepita that symbol, that ethereal and insubstantial image, that sum and substance of all I can love beneath God, in God, and subordinated to God, I must think of her as dead, as Beatrice was dead when Dante sang of her.

If I leave her among the living, I can never succeed in making her a pure idea; and so, to make her a pure idea, I murder her in my mind.

Then I weep for her, then I am horrified at my crime, and

---

[29] *Beatrice Portinari, ideal and inspiration of Dante from the age of nine until his death.*

I go to her in spirit, and with the warmth of my heart I bring her back to life, and I see her, not vague and diaphanous, almost diffused among rose-colored clouds and celestial flowers, as the fiery Ghibeline saw his beloved on a peak in Purgatory, but corporeal, solid, well-defined in the serene, clear atmosphere, like the most perfect works of Greek sculpture; like Galatea, brought to life by Pygmalion's love, stepping down from her marble pedestal, full of life, breathing love, glowing in her youth and beauty.[30]

From the bottom of my tormented heart I cry then: "My virtue is fallen away. Do not forsake me, O my God. Hasten to my aid. Show me Thy face and I shall be saved."

Thus I recover my strength to resist temptation. Thus the hope that I may return to the old peace of mind as soon as I leave this place is reborn in me.

The Devil strives furiously to swallow the pure waters of Jordan, which are the people consecrated to God. He calls up Hell against them, and unchains all his monsters. Saint Bonaventure has said: "We should not wonder that these people sinned, but rather that they did not sin." In the end, I shall know how to resist and not sin. God is watching over me.

June 6.

Pepita's old nurse, now her housekeeper, is like a good piece of wrinkled cloth, Father says. She is talkative, gay, and more clever than most people. She married the son of Master Cencias and she inherited from her father-in-law what the son did not: an amazing facility for the arts and crafts. But with a difference: Master Cencias could make a screw-pin for a wine-

---

[30] *The sculptor Pygmalion formed a statue of a girl so beautiful that he fell in love with it. He prayed the statue might come alive, and his prayer was answered by Aphrodite who gave life to Galatea.*

press, straighten the wheels of a cart, or make a plow, while this daughter-in-law of his makes sweets, syrups, and other confections. The father-in-law exercised the useful arts; the daughter-in-law those of pleasure, albeit an innocent, or at any rate a permissible, pleasure.

Antonoña, as she is called, enjoys or has arrogated to herself a relationship of familiarity with all the gentry. She is in and out of every house as if it were her own. She uses the familiar form of address with all the young gentlemen and ladies of Pepita's age, or four or five years older; she calls them boys and girls, and treats them all as though she had nursed them at her breast.

She speaks to me as familiarly as to all the others. She comes to see me, she enters my room, and several times now she has told me I am an ingrate, and that I do wrong in not going to see her lady.

Father, all unawares, accuses me of being odd in my ways; he calls me unsociable, and he, too, insists that I go back to the gatherings. Last night I couldn't stand up to his repeated insistence, and I went very early, as Father was leaving to go over his accounts with the overseer.

Would that I had not gone!

Pepita was alone. We both blushed when we saw each other and exchanged greetings. Our hands met shyly, without a word.

I did not press her hand; she did not press mine, but we held them clasped for a moment.

The look Pepita gave me was not one of love, only friendship, sympathy, and a deep sadness.

She had divined all my inner conflict; she assumed that sacred love had triumphed in my soul, that my resolution not to love her was firm and invincible.

She did not venture to complain of me; she knew I was in the right. A barely audible sigh, which escaped from her fresh, parted lips, indicated how deeply she deplored it.

Our hands were still joined. We were both silent. How was I to tell her that she was not for me, nor I for her; that we had to separate forever?

Although I did not tell her so in words, I did say it with my eyes. My stern look confirmed her fears, convinced her of the verdict from which there was no appeal.

Suddenly her eyes clouded over; her whole lovely face, now pale with a translucent pallor, contracted in a beautiful expression of melancholy. She looked like the Mother of Sorrows. Tears slowly filled her eyes and began to run down her cheeks.

I don't know what happened to me. Or how can I describe it even if I knew?

I brought my lips to her face to dry her tears, and our mouths met in a kiss.

An ineffable rapture, a weakness fraught with danger invaded my whole being and hers. She swooned, and I held her in my arms.

Heaven so willed it that we heard the footsteps and the cough of the approaching Vicar, and we sprang apart.

Coming to myself, and summoning all the strength of my will, I managed to fill that terrible silent scene with the words I spoke in a low, intense voice: "The first and the last!"

I was alluding to that profane kiss; but as if my words were an evocation, the vision of the Apocalypse appeared before my mind in all its terrible majesty. I saw that it was in actual fact the first and the last. With the two-edged sword that had issued from her mouth I scourged my soul, so full of evil, of vice, and of sin.

I spent that whole evening in a frenzy, in an inner delirium that I don't know how I managed to conceal.

I left Pepita's house very early.

When I was alone, my bitterness grew even greater.

As I recalled that kiss and those words of farewell, I compared myself to the traitor Judas who sold his Lord with a kiss, and to the bloody and treacherous murderer, Joab,[31] who buried the sharp steel in Abner's entrails even as he kissed him.

I have committed two treacherous and false acts.

I have failed both God and her.

I am an abominable creature.

June 11.

There is still time to set everything right. Pepita will recover from her love and forget that weakness which overcame us both.

I have not gone back to her house since that night.

Antonoña does not come to mine.

By dint of my pleas, I have obtained my father's formal promise that we shall leave here on the 25th, after Saint John's day, which is celebrated here with fireworks and a famous vigil on the eve.

Away from Pepita, I am growing calmer and I believe that perhaps this dawning of love has been a proving-ground for me.

All these nights I have prayed; I have stayed awake; I have greatly mortified the flesh.

The insistence of my supplications, the deep contrition in my heart have found grace before the Lord, and he has shown me His great mercy.

The Lord has sent down fire into the fortress of my spirit,

---

[31] *Joab was King David's nephew and an officer in his army. David forgave him his treacherous murder of Abner because of his administrative ability.*

as the Prophet says; He has enlightened my reason; He has set afire the core of my will, and has shown me the way.

This act of divine love, deriving from the Supreme Will, has brought me at moments, unworthy though I am, to genuinely tranquil prayer. I have stripped away all human images from the uttermost depths of my soul, even to the image of that woman; and unless pride blinds me, I believe I have found and enjoyed, in peace of mind and heart, the supreme goodness lying in the soul's central core.

Alongside this goodness, all else is evil; face to face with this beauty, all else is ugly; compared with this happiness, all else is misfortune; before this loftiness, all else is base. Who would not forget and despise all other loves for the love of God?

Yes, the profane image of that woman will quit my soul finally and forever. I shall make of my prayers and penance a scourge with which to drive her from it, as Christ drove the moneylenders from the temple.

June 18.

This is the last letter I shall be writing to you.

I'll be leaving here on the 25th without fail. I shall have the pleasure of embracing you.

At your side I shall be better. You will give me the courage and lend me the energy I lack.

At the moment my heart is a storm of conflicting emotions.

The disorder of my ideas must be evident from the disorder of my writing.

Twice I have gone back to Pepita's house. I have been cold and stern, as it was right that I should; but at what a cost!

Yesterday Father told me that Pepita is indisposed and is not at home to callers.

Instantly the thought came to me that her ill-requited love might be the cause of her indisposition.

Why did I return the fiery glances she gave me? Why did I deceive her so vilely? Why did I make her think I loved her? Why did my vile mouth seek hers, burning and burning her with the fires of hell?

No, my sin must not bring another sin in its wake.

What was done cannot be undone; but it can and must be set right.

I repeat that I shall leave without fail on the 25th.

The bold Antonoña has just marched in to see me.

I hid this letter, as though it were wrong to write to you. Antonoña was here only a moment.

I stood up to speak to her so that the visit could be cut short.

During the few moments she was here, she uttered a thousand absurdities that have upset me and pained me.

Finally, as she was leaving, she exclaimed in her half-gypsy jargon, "Go on, love-cheat, rascal. Curse you; may mad dogs rip your skin for making my girl sick. You're killing her with your blowing hot and cold."

With that, the fiendish woman pinched me hard on the shoulders five or six times, in a most unseemly and vulgar way, as if she longed to tear the skin off me in strips. Then she went away, throwing off sparks.

I am not complaining; I deserve this brutal joke, if it was a joke. I deserve to be tormented by demons with red-hot tongs.

O my God, grant that Pepita may forget me; grant that, if need be, she may fall in love with another man, and be happy with him.

Can I ask for anything more, my God?

Father knows nothing; suspects nothing. It is better so.

Good-bye, until a few days from now, when we shall see and embrace each other.

How changed you will find me! How full of bitterness my heart is! How lost my innocence! How wounded and lacerated my soul!

II

FIRST AND SECOND CHRONICLES

These letters we have transcribed are the only ones from Don Luis de Vargas. We should be left in ignorance of the outcome of this love affair, and this simple, impassioned chronicle would remain incomplete, if a person, fully acquainted with the whole affair, had not written the narrative that follows.

* * *

No one in the village wondered at Pepita's indisposition, much less thought of looking for the cause, known until now only to us, to her, Don Luis, the Dean, and the discreet Antonoña.

On the contrary, many people may have been wondering at Pepita's gay life, her daily at-homes, even at the jaunts to the country that had been going on for some time. So it seemed entirely natural that Pepita should return to her customary retirement.

Her love for Don Luis, so silent and deep-rooted, had been concealed from the prying eyes of Doña Casilda, Currito, and all the persons in the village whom Don Luis had named in his letters. How much less, then, must the other people have known. It never entered anyone's head, no one ever dreamed that the "theologian," the "saint," as they called Don Luis, could be his own father's rival, and that he could have accomplished what the strong and forceful Don Pedro de Vargas had not been able to accomplish, awakening the love of that pretty, elegant, aloof, and inscrutable widow.

Despite the familiar footing on which the village ladies and their servants live, Pepita had never let her household infer a thing. Only Antoñona, sharp-eyed as a lynx about everything, and especially what had to do with her nursling's concerns, had divined the mystery.

Antoñona did not keep her discovery from Pepita, and Pepita could not deny the truth to the woman who had nursed her, who idolized her. Even though she prided herself on finding out and gossiping about everything that took place in the village, she was close-mouthed and loyal to the core in all that mattered to her mistress.

So it came about that Antoñona became Pepita's confidante, and Pepita found comfort in unburdening her heart to one who, though vulgar and rude in her expressions and language, was not so in the feelings and ideas she expressed and formulated.

Antoñona's visits to Don Luis, her words, and even the fierce, disrespectful, and unseemly pinches that bruised his flesh and outraged his dignity the last time she went to see him can be explained on these grounds.

Not only had Pepita not urged Antoñona to carry messages to Don Luis; she did not even know her old nurse had done so.

Antoñona had taken matters into her own hands and had assigned herself a rôle in this affair entirely on her own initiative.

She found out everything with marvelous perspicacity, as has already been said.

At a time when Pepita herself was scarcely aware that she was in love with Don Luis, Antoñona already knew it. Pepita had hardly begun to send him those ardent, secret, and involuntary glances that shook him so severely and that not one of the company present had seen, when Antonoña, who was not there, mentioned them to Pepita. And hardly had her glances been softly returned than Antonoña knew that, too.

Accordingly, the lady had little to confide to a maid so shrewd and clairvoyant concerning everything that was taking place in the most hidden recesses of her heart.

* * *

Our narrative begins five days after the date of the last letter.

It was eleven o'clock in the morning. Pepita was in an upstairs sitting room adjoining her bedroom and dressing room, where no one except Antonoña ever entered unless summoned by her.

The furnishings of the room she was in were unpretentious, although comfortable and clean. The curtains and upholstery on the armchairs, sofas, and easy chairs were of flowered chintz. Writing materials and paper lay on a small mahogany table; and numerous religious and historical books stood in a bookcase, also of mahogany. The walls were decorated with prints of religious subjects, but revealing good taste unheard of, rare, almost incredible for a village in Andalusia. The prints were not poor French lithographs, but products of our own engravers, such as the Marvel of Sicily by Rafael; the Saint Ildefonso and the Virgin, the Conception, and the Saint Bernard and the two Lunettes, by Murillo.

A portable writing desk, or escritoire, inlaid with shell, mother-of-pearl, ivory, and bronze stood upon an antique oak table, supported by spiral columns, beside many small boxes where Pepita kept her accounts and other papers. On the same table, two porcelain vases were filled with flowers. Three gilded cages of canaries and linnets, and some pottery plant-holders from the Sevillian Carthusian monastery hung from the wall, holding ivy geraniums and other plants.

That room was Pepita's retreat, which only the doctor and the Vicar were permitted to enter during the day. Early in the evening her overseer used to come to render his accounts. The room was an office and was so called.

Pepita was half sitting, half reclining, on a sofa beside which was a small table holding several books.

She had just got up and was wearing a light summer wrapper. Her blonde hair, still uncombed, seemed the more beautiful for its disorder, and her face, pale and with eyes darkly circled, though young, smooth, and fresh, looked the lovelier for the illness that had robbed her of her color.

Pepita was showing signs of impatience; she was obviously expecting someone.

Finally the person she was awaiting came in without announcing himself. It was the Vicar.

After the usual greetings, the conversation began as soon as the Vicar was comfortably seated in an easy chair beside Pepita.

"I'm glad you called me, my daughter, but you needn't have bothered, for I was going to come to see you in any case. You're pale! What's the matter? Is there something important you have to tell me?"

Pepita answered this series of affectionate queries with a deep sigh. Then she said, "Can't you guess what my illness is? Can't you see the cause of my suffering?"

The Vicar shrugged, staring at Pepita with some alarm. He knew nothing, but he was surprised at the vehemence with which she spoke.

Pepita went on: "Father, I should not have called you. I

should have gone to the church to speak to you in the confessional, and confess my sins. But unfortunately I am not repentant; my heart is hardened in its evil, and I have had neither the courage nor the inclination to talk to my confessor. I'd rather talk to my friend."

"What's this you're saying about sins and hardness of heart? Are you mad? What sins could a good woman like you have committed?"

"No, Father, I am bad. I've been deceiving you, deceiving myself, trying to deceive God."

"Come, come. Calm down. Speak with order and judgment, and stop talking nonsense."

"How else can I talk when I am possessed by the spirit of evil?"

"Holy Mother of God! Don't be a fool, child. See here, my daughter, three are the devils most to be feared who can enter the soul, and I feel sure that none of them can have dared to approach yours. One is Leviathan, or the spirit of pride; another is Mammon, or the spirit of avarice; the third is Asmodeus, or the spirit of impure love."

"Then I am the victim of all three; all three possess me."

"How dreadful! . . . Once more I urge you to be calm. What you're the victim of is delirium."

"Would to God I were! But, alas, the opposite is the case. I'm avaricious, because I own an abundance of property, and fail to perform the charitable works I should; I'm proud, for I have disdained many men, not because of virtue, not because of chastity, but because I did not consider them worthy of my affection. God has punished me; God has permitted that third enemy you mentioned to take possession of me."

"What are you saying, child? What kind of bedevilment has come over you? Are you in love, by any chance? And if you are, where is the harm in that? Aren't you free? Get married,

then, and stop your foolishness. I'm sure that my friend Don
Pedro de Vargas has wrought the miracle. The demon is none
other than Don Pedro! I declare I'm astonished! I never thought
the matter was so ripe and advanced as all that."

"But it's not Don Pedro de Vargas I'm in love with."

"Well, who is it, then?"

Pepita rose from her sofa and went to the door. She
opened it and looked out to see if anyone were listening on the
other side of it; then closed it again. Then she went up to the
Vicar and deeply distressed, with trembling voice, and tear-
filled eyes, said almost in the old man's ear:

"I'm hopelessly in love with his son."

"With what son?" cried the Vicar, who did not yet wish
to believe her.

"What son would it be? I'm madly, frantically in love with
Don Luis."

Consternation and the most dolorous astonishment were
painted on the face of the simple, affectionate priest.

After a moment's pause, the Vicar said, "But that is a hope-
less love, an impossible love. Don Luis can't be in love with
you."

A ray of happiness shone through the tears dimming
Pepita's beautiful eyes. Her lovely, fresh mouth, drawn in sadness, opened sweetly, giving a glimpse of her white teeth and
shaping into a smile.

"He is in love with me," said Pepita in a tone of poorly
disguised satisfaction which triumphed over her depression
and her pangs of conscience.

At her words the consternation and astonishment of the
Vicar knew no limits. If the saint of his deepest devotion had
been cast down from the altar, and had fallen at his feet in a
hundred thousand pieces, the Vicar could not have been more
dismayed. He kept staring at Pepita with incredulity, as if

doubting that it could be the truth and not an hallucination born of feminine vanity. His belief in the sanctity and mysticism of Don Luis was that firm.

"He does love me," Pepita repeated in answer to his incredulous stare.

"Women are worse than the devil!" cried the Vicar. "You could outfox the very demon himself."

"Didn't I tell you I'm very wicked?"

"God help us! Come now, be calm. God's mercy is infinite. Tell me what has happened."

"What could have happened? I love him; I adore him; he loves me too, even though he is struggling to stifle his love and may perhaps succeed. And you're very much to blame, without knowing it."

"That is the last straw! What do you mean that I am very much to blame?"

"With your characteristic goodness you've done nothing but praise Don Luis to me, and I know for a fact that you've heaped even greater praises of me on Don Luis, though far less deserved. What was bound to happen then? Am I made of iron? Am I an old woman at twenty?"

"You're right. You are absolutely right. What a fool I am. I've contributed greatly to this work of Lucifer's."

The Vicar was such a good and humble man that as he spoke he became as confused and contrite as if he were the criminal and Pepita the judge.

Pepita recognized her utter selfishness in making the Vicar an accomplice, almost the principal agent of her lapse, and she said to him: "Don't be upset, Father; for God's sake, don't be upset. You see how perverse I am? I commit the worst sins and then try to make you, the best and most virtuous of men, responsible for them. It wasn't your praise of Don Luis to me, but my own eyes and my own lack of modesty that have undone me. Even if you had never mentioned to me Don Luis's endowments, his knowledge, his talent, and his warm heart, I would have found out all about them on my own account, merely by listening to him talk, for, after all, I'm not so stupid and uncouth. I've noticed, too, how gallant he is, his inborn refinement and the unstudied elegance of his manners, his eyes full of fire and intelligence. In a word, he seems to me altogether lovable and desirable. Your eulogies of him have served only to flatter my good taste, not to awaken it. I was enchanted by your praise of him because it coincided with my own opinion, and was like the beguiling echo, muted and softened, of what I myself was thinking. Your most eloquent panegyric of Don Luis comes nowhere near those I have uttered in my heart, wordlessly, every minute, every second."

"Don't work yourself up, daughter," the Vicar interrupted.

Pepita went on with increasing excitement: "But, what a difference between your praises and my thoughts! You delineated what you saw in Don Luis—the model and example of a priest, a missionary, an evangelist; now preaching the Gospel in distant lands and converting the heathen, now laboring in Spain to make of Christianity a reality that has been lost today through the impiety of some, and the lack of virtue, charity, and knowledge in others. In contrast, I pictured him as a suitor, in love with me, forgetting God for me, dedicating his life to me, yielding me his soul, becoming my rod and my staff, my beloved companion. I've longed to commit a sacrilegious theft. I've dreamed of stealing him from God and His temple, like the thief, the enemy of heaven who stole the richest jewel from the sacred monstrance. In order to commit this robbery, I cast aside my widow's weeds and my mourning for my mother, and dressed myself in gay and worldly garments. I came out of my retirement and sought and surrounded myself with people. I've tried to make myself beautiful; I've looked after this miserable body of mine with diabolical care—this body that will go down to the grave and become vile dust. And finally I've sent Don Luis provocative glances, and as I took his hand, I've tried to transmit from my veins to his this inextinguishable fire that is consuming me."

"Ah, child, child! How much all that you are saying hurts me! Who could even have imagined it?"

"But that's not all," Pepita added. "I've succeeded in making Don Luis love me. He has told me so with his eyes. Yes, his love is as deep, as ardent as mine. His virtue, his aspiration to treasures not of this world, his manly strength, have all gone into the struggle to conquer this insane passion. I've tried to obstruct him. Once, after he had been absent from this house for several days, he came to see me and found me alone. As I offered him my hand, tears rose in my eyes. The devil inspired me to an accursed, mute eloquence. I made him understand without a word my sorrow at his rejection of me because he could not love me, because he set another, immaculate love above mine. That broke down his resistance to temptation, and he lowered his mouth to my face, to dry my tears. Ours mouths met. If God had not so willed it that you should arrive at that very moment what would have become of me?"

"What a shame, my daughter! What a shame!" the Vicar said.

Pepita covered her face with both hands and began to sob like a Magdalen. The hands were indeed beautiful, more beautiful than Don Luis had said in his letters. Their whiteness, their clear translucency, the tapering fingers, the polished, shining rosiness of the pearly nails were enough to drive any man mad.

In spite of his eighty years, the good Vicar understood how Don Luis had stumbled or fallen.

"Don't take on so, girl!" he exclaimed. "Don't break my heart! Be calm. Doubtless Don Luis has repented of his sin. You repent, too, and it will all be over. God will forgive you and make saints of you both. When Don Luis leaves day after tomorrow, that will be a clear indication that virtue has triumphed in him, and that he is fleeing from you, as he should, to do penance for his sin, to keep his promise, and to take up his vocation."

"That's all very well," Pepita replied, "to keep his promise . . . to take up his vocation . . . and to kill me first! Why did he love me, why did he encourage me, why did he deceive me? His kiss was a seal, like a branding-iron with which he marked and sealed me as his slave. And now that I am branded and enslaved, he leaves me, he betrays me, he murders me. A fine beginning for his missions, his preachings, and his evangelistic triumphs! It shall not be! Before God, it shall not be!"

This outburst of anger and of love's wrath struck the Vicar speechless.

Pepita had risen to her feet. Her bearing, her gestures, revealed the tragic stirring of her spirit. Her eyes were gleaming like daggers, shining like twin suns. The Vicar said nothing as he stared at her almost with terror. She was pacing the room with long strides, no longer looking like a shy gazelle, but rather like an enraged lioness.

"Well, then," she said, facing the Vicar anew, "shall he be permitted to make fun of me, to break my heart, to humiliate it, to trample it underfoot after deceitfully robbing me of it? He'll have good cause to remember me! He'll answer to me for it! If he's so saintly, if he's so virtuous, why did he look at me and promise me everything with his eyes? If he loves God so much, why does he harm one of God's creatures? Is that loving-kindness? Is that religion? No; it's heartless selfishness."

Pepita's anger could not last long. With her last words, it turned to dejection and she collapsed into an armchair, crying harder than before, with genuine anguish.

The Vicar felt the tenderest compassion for her; but when he saw that his adversary was yielding, he regained his vigor. "Pepita, child," he said, "pull yourself together. Don't torture yourself like this. Think how hard he must have struggled to conquer himself; he has not deceived you. He loves you with all his heart, but God and duty come first with him. You will learn that this life is brief and soon done. You will be united in heaven, there to love each other as the angels love. God will accept your sacrifice, and reward and repay you with interest. Even your pride should be satisfied. Think of what you are worth to have caused a man like Don Luis to hesitate and even to sin! Think what a deep wound you've made in his heart! Be content with that. Be generous, be brave! Rival him in firmness. Let him go. Tear the fire of an impure love from your breast. Love him as your neighbor, for the love of God. Keep his image in your mind, but as that of one of the chosen who reserves the noblest portion of his soul to his Creator. I hardly know what I'm saying to you, daughter, for I'm deeply perturbed; but as you are a woman of great intelligence and discretion, you will understand my babblings. In addition to everything else, there are strong worldly reasons which would oppose this absurd love affair, even if Don Luis's vocation and his vow were not opposed to it. His father has been courting you; he has aspired to your hand, even though you don't love him. What would people think if it were to come out now that the son was his father's rival? Wouldn't the father be angry with the son because of you? Consider how appalling this all is, and for the sake of Christ Crucified and his blessed mother, Most Holy Mary, control yourself."

"It's easy for you to give advice!" Pepita answered, slightly calmer. "But how hard for me to follow it, when it is as though a tempest were unleashed in my mind! I'm even afraid I'll go mad."

"The advice I'm giving you is for your own good. Let Don Luis go. Absence is the best cure for the pangs of love. He'll get over his passion by devoting himself to his studies and dedicating himself to the altar. Little by little, you, too, will find peace, once Don Luis has gone, and you'll retain only a pleasant, wistful memory of him, which will not hurt you. He will be like a beautiful poem that will gild your life with its light. Suppose all your wishes were granted. Earthly loves seldom last. The delight which the imagination envisions, even when enjoyed and drained to the lees, is as nothing compared with the bitter dregs it leaves. How much better that your love—almost uncontaminated, hardly sullied—should be lost and evaporated as it rises like clouds of incense to heaven, than that, once satisfied, it should die of satiety! Be strong enough to take the cup from your lips before you've done more than barely taste the wine within it. Make of this wine a libation and an offering to the Divine Redeemer. He, in turn, will give you of the drink He offered to the Samaritan—a drink that never palls, that will slake your thirst and bring eternal life."

"Father! Father! How good you are! Your inspired words give me courage. I will control myself; I will conquer myself. It would indeed be shameful, wouldn't it, if Luis were able to control and conquer himself, while I prove too weak to conquer myself? Let him go. He's leaving day after tomorrow. Let him go with God. See, here's his card. He came with his father yesterday to say good-bye to me, but I didn't receive him. I won't see him any more now. I don't even want to keep the poetic memory of which you spoke. This love has been a nightmare. I will cast it far from me."

"Good, very good. This is the way I like to see you, full of energy and courage."

"Ah, Father! God has struck down my pride with this blow; my vanity was so insolent, and that man's disdain was needed to humble me as I deserve to be humbled . . . How could I be more prostrate or more resigned? Luis is right; I don't deserve him. How could I raise myself to him however much I might try? How could I understand him? How could my spirit find perfect communication with his? I'm an ignorant villager, untutored, stupid; while he understands every field of learning; he has a knowledge of all hidden wisdom; he has scaled the peaks of the world of the mind. He can rise to the heights on the wings of his genius, leaving me here below, powerless to follow him with even my faintest hope, my most disconsolate sighs."

"By the wounds of Christ, Pepita, don't say that, or even think it. Don Luis does not look down on you as uncouth, nor think himself so wise that you don't understand him, nor any of the rest of that nonsense you're saying! He's going away because he must keep his promise to God. And you ought to be glad he's going, because you'll get over your love, and God will reward you for your great sacrifice."

Pepita, who had stopped crying and had dried her tears with her handkerchief, replied calmly: "Very well, Father; I shall be glad. I'm almost glad now that he's going. I long for tomorrow to pass, and then for Antoñona to come and tell me when I wake up on the following day, 'Don Luis has left.' You'll see how peace and my old serenity will come back to my heart."

"So be it," said the Vicar. And convinced that he had wrought a miracle in virtually curing Pepita of her illness, he said good-bye to her and went home, unable to resist a pleasant touch of vanity at the thought of the influence he exerted over the noble spirit of that lovely girl.

* * *

Pepita had risen to accompany the Vicar to the door. No sooner had she closed it behind him and was alone in the middle of the room than she stood motionless a while, staring unseeingly before her with tearless eyes. She might have reminded a poet or an artist of the figure of Ariadne,[32] as Catullus describes her after her abandonment by Theseus on the Island of Naxos. Suddenly, as though a knot around her throat had been undone, as if a cord strangling her had snapped, Pepita burst into piteous sobs, shaken by a storm of weeping, and her body, so lovely and delicate, sank down on the cold tiles. There on the floor, her face in her hands, her hair dishevelled, and her dress in disorder, she kept on sobbing and moaning.

She might have stayed there indefinitely if Antoñona had not come. Before she came in and saw her, Antoñona could hear the grieving of her mistress, and she dashed into the room. She saw Pepita lying on the floor, and flew into a rage.

"Look at that!" she said. "Look how that sponger, that blackguard, that old rascal, that fool consoles his friends! He's been up to some mischief; he's probably dealt this little darling of mine a couple of hard blows. Then he goes off and leaves her here half dead. Back he goes to the church, where he'll get out his traps and get ready to say the funeral service, and to throw holy water around, and bury her on me, just like that."

Antoñona must have been about forty, a bustling woman, hardworking and stronger than many a ditch-digger. She would

---

[32] *Ariadne, daughter of Minos, king of Crete, led Theseus out of the Labyrinth after he had killed the Minotaur. She sailed with him from Crete, but he abandoned her on the island of Naxos.*

frequently lift with little more than the strength of her hands a wineskin containing seventy-five pounds of oil or wine, and set it on the back of a mule, or take a sack of wheat and carry it up to the granary in the loft. Though Pepita was no feather, Antonoña picked her up from the floor in her arms as easily as she would a bag of down. She laid her tenderly on the sofa, like one setting down the most delicate and fragile ornament with great care so as not to break it.

"What kind of a fit of grief is this?" asked Antonoña. "I bet anything that booby of a Vicar preached you a sermon like gall, and broke your heart with reproaches."

Pepita went on crying and sobbing without answering.

"Now, now! Stop that crying and tell me what's the matter. What did the Vicar say?"

"He didn't say anything to offend me," Pepita answered at length.

Seeing then that Antonoña was eagerly waiting for her to speak, and feeling the need to unburden herself to the one closest to her, the one who understood her in the most completely human terms, Pepita began to speak.

"The Vicar gently scolded me. He urged me to repent of my sins; to let Don Luis go in peace; to be happy over his leaving; to forget him. I said yes to everything. I promised to be glad Don Luis is leaving. I wanted then to forget him and even to hate him. But, you see, Antonoña, I can't. That's an undertaking beyond my strength. While the Vicar was here, I felt I had the heart for anything; but no sooner had he left than I lost my courage and collapsed, as if God had forsaken me. I had been dreaming of a happy life with this man I love; I was picturing myself raised to his level through the miracle of love; fancying my poor mind in perfect communion with his sublime intelligence; my will at one with his, both of us sharing the same thoughts; our hearts joined in the same accord.

But God is taking him away from me and carrying him off, and I'm left alone without hope or consolation. Isn't that terrible? Isn't it really? The Vicar's reasoning is just and prudent . . . He did convince me for the moment. But then he left, and all the value of his reasoning seemed to me nil; a vain play of words; lies, snares, and tricks. I love Don Luis, which is a reason stronger than any other. Why doesn't he leave everything and come to me, if he loves me? Why doesn't he come to me and break his vows and annul his commitments? I never knew before what it is to love. Now I know; nothing on earth or in heaven is stronger. What wouldn't I do for Don Luis? Yet he does nothing for me. Perhaps he doesn't love me. No, Don Luis can't be in love with me. I've been deceiving myself, letting my vanity blind me. If Don Luis loved me, he would sacrifice his plans, his vows, his good name, his aspirations to sainthood and to becoming a luminary of the Church; he would sacrifice everything. God forgive me . . . what I'm about to say is terrible, but it's what I feel here in my breast; it's burning here, on my fevered forehead: I'd give even the salvation of my soul for him."

"Jesus, Mary, and Joseph!" Antonoña interposed.

"It's true. Blessed Mother of Sorrows, forgive me, forgive me, . . . I'm mad . . . I don't know what I'm saying, and here I am blaspheming."

"Yes, my child, you're thinking evil thoughts. God help us, how that coxcomb of a theologian has warped your judgment! Well, if I were you, I wouldn't take it out on heaven, which is not to blame; I'd take it out on that jackanapes of a seminarian. I'd pay him back or my name wouldn't be Antonoña. I've got a good notion to go after him and drag him here by the ear. I'd make him beg your pardon, and kiss your feet on his knees."

"No, Antonoña. I see that my madness is contagious and that you're raving, too. There's nothing to be done, after all, but what the Vicar has advised me to do. And I'll do it, if it kills me. If I die for him, he'll love me, he'll keep the picture of me in his memory, and my love in his heart; and God in His goodness will permit me to see him again in heaven, with the eyes of the soul. There our spirits can love and be united with each other."

Though she was strong-fibred and far from sentimental, Antonoña felt tears rise to her eyes when she heard this. "Lord, child," she said, "you're going to make me turn on the water-works and bawl like a calf. Calm down now, and don't talk about dying, even as a joke. I can see your nerves are all strung up tight. Do you want me to fetch you a cup of linden-flower tea?"

"No, thank you . . . You may go now . . . You can see I'm myself again."

"I'll close the windows. Try to get some sleep now. You haven't had any sleep for days. No wonder you're like this. Damn that Don Luis and all his nonsense about being a priest! He's given you a rude awakening."

Pepita had closed her eyes. She was lying quiet and calm, and was tired of talking to Antonoña.

The maid, thinking she was asleep, or that she would like to go to sleep, bent over Pepita, dropped a long, soft kiss on her white forehead, arranged and folded her gown around her, adjusted the windows to leave the room in semi-darkness, and went out on tiptoe, closing the door without a sound.

* * *

While these things were happening in Pepita's house, Don Luis de Vargas was no happier or calmer in his.

His father, who almost never let a day go by without a trip on horseback to the country, had wanted to take Luis with him. But Luis had excused himself, saying he had a headache, so Don Pedro went without him. Almost all of Luis's morning had been given over to melancholy thoughts, though he was as firm as a rock in his resolution to wipe the image of Pepita from his soul and to dedicate himself completely to God.

Nonetheless, it must not be thought that he did not love the young widow. From his letters, we have already seen the vehemence of his passion, but with the same pious intentions and lofty considerations expounded in them, and which we may omit so as not to be guilty of prolixity, he continued to keep his feelings under close control.

Perhaps, if we were to delve deeply into this affair, we might discover that the vow inwardly taken, though not yet carried out, was not his only source of conflict; there was the love of God, respect for his father, whose rival he did not wish to be, and, finally, the vocation he felt for the priesthood.

There were still other motives, less flawless and of a lower degree of purity. Don Luis was tenacious; he was stubborn; he had that quality which, well directed, constitutes what is called strength of character; and nothing could diminish him more in his own eyes than to change his mind or his habits. The objectives of his entire life, which he had avowed and declared to whomever he came in contact with, his moral stature, in a word, which was that of an aspirant to sainthood, of a man consecrated to God, of a person imbued with the most exalted religious philosophy—all this could not be sloughed off without great detriment to his self-esteem, as would be the case if he let himself be carried away by his love for Pepita Jiménez. He considered that if he yielded, he would be on a par with Esau, selling his birthright, and dimming his glory, although the price was incomparably higher.

In general, we human are the puppets of circumstance; we let ourselves be carried along by the current; we seldom ad-

dress ourselves undeviatingly to a single end. We do not choose
our rôles; we play as best we can that which blind Fortune has
allotted us. The entire life of many men, their profession, their
political affiliation, hangs on accident, chance, the unexpected
quirk of Fortune.

Don Luis's pride rebelled against all this with titanic
strength. What would people say about him? Above all, what
would he think of himself, if the ideal of his life, the new man
he had fashioned in his soul, all his plans for a life of virtue,
honor, and even sainthood were to vanish in an instant, to melt
in the warmth of a glance, in the flickering flame of a pair of
beautiful eyes, like frost in the still weak rays of the morning
sun?

These and other selfish reasons, as well as legitimate and
sound considerations, arranged themselves against the widow.
But as all his reasons wore the same religious habit, he was
unable to recognize them and distinguish among them. He believed his love of self to be the love of God, as well as what
really was the love of God. For example, he summoned to mind
the lives of many saints who had withstood temptations greater
than his, and he did not want to be less than they. In particular, he recalled the rectitude of Saint John Chrysostom,
who had found the strength to reject his good and loving
mother's pleas not to leave her and become a priest, despite
her tears, her gentle plaints, all her eloquent and sensible arguments, even when she led him to her own room and made him
sit down next to the bed in which she had brought him into
the world. After concentrating on that example, Luis could not
let himself fail to reject the pleas of a strange woman whom he
had met such a short time ago, nor go on vacillating between
his duty and the attractions of a young woman perhaps flirting
more than actually in love.

Don Luis next considered the sublimity and dignity of the

priesthood to which he had been called, and it seemed to him far above all the institutions and the miserable crowns of the earth. For its Founder had been no mortal man, no volatile and servile populace, no irruption or invention of a barbaric people, no violent and rebellious hosts motivated by avarice, no angel, no archangel, no created power, but the Paraclete[33] Himself. How could he cast aside that august dignity, that power which God had granted not even to the archangels nearest His throne, for the sake of a frivolous excitement aroused by a girl, for the sake of a tiny, perhaps a feigned tear? How could he step down to mingle with the obscure masses, how become one of the flock after dreaming that he would be their shepherd, that he would bind and unbind on earth what God might bind and unbind in Heaven, that he would remit sins, regenerate the people through water and the soul; indoctrinate them in the name of an infallible authority; passing judgments that the Most High would later ratify and confirm; become the initiator and agent of august mysteries inaccessible to human reason; and call down from Heaven, not the fire that consumes the victim, as Elias did, but the Holy Ghost, the word made flesh, and the flood of grace that cleanses the heart and leaves it pure as gold?

As Luis reflected upon all such matters, his spirit was uplifted, elevated above the clouds to the empyrean, while poor Pepita Jiménez remained far below, hardly visible to him.

But soon his imagination faltered in its flight, and his soul returned to earth. Then he saw Pepita again, so charming, so young, so ingenuous, and so much in love, and again Pepita began to contend in his heart against his stronger, most fixed plans, and Luis feared they would tumble and fall.

* * *

---

[33] *A title of the Holy Ghost, with the meaning of "Comforter" or "Advocate."*

Luis was thus being tossed about by warring thoughts when Currito came into his room without so much as a by-your-leave.

Currito who didn't think much of his cousin as long as he was nothing but a theological student, had come to respect and admire him beyond all reason ever since he had seen him master Lucifer.

To know theology but not how to ride had discredited Luis in Currito's eyes. But when Currito realized that in addition to possessing book-learning and all that he himself could not understand (though he supposed it to be difficult and involved) Luis was able to keep his seat so gallantly on the back of a spirited animal, his respect and affection for Luis knew no bounds. Currito was a lazy fellow, a wastrel, an inanimate object, really, but he had an affectionate and loyal heart. Currito's idol, Luis, treated him as all superior beings treat the inferiors who are fond of them. He let himself be loved, that is to say, he was despotically ruled by Currito in matters of slight importance.

"I came by for you," he said, "to go to the Casino with me. It's lively today and full of people. What are you doing here alone, fooling around like a ninny?"

Luis barely answered him, but as if acting under orders, he picked up his hat and stick, saying, "Wherever you wish," and followed Currito, who went ahead, highly pleased with the domination he exercised.

The Casino was indeed crammed with people, owing to the importance of the following day, which was St. John's festival.[34] In addition to the village gentry, many outsiders from nearby villages who had come to take part in the festival and the night's gathering were there.

The crowd had gathered in the marble-tiled patio, where

---

[34] June 24th.

a fountain was playing in the center, and pots of four o'clocks, roses, carnations, and sweet basil stood. An awning of heavy canvas covered the patio to shade it from the sun. An arcade, or cloister, supported by marble columns, surrounded it, and both in the arcade and the many rooms opening off it, there were card tables, magazine and newspaper racks, tables for coffee or refreshments, and chairs, benches and a few arm-chairs. Frequent whitewashing kept the walls glistening like snow and there was no dearth of pictures to adorn them—mainly French colored lithographs with appropriate bilingual captions beneath them. Some represented the life of Napoleon I, from Toulon to Saint Helena; others the adventures of Ma-thilde[35] and Malek-Adel; others, the Templar's exploits in love and war; Rebecca, Lady Rowena and Ivanhoe; and still others, the flirtations, the pranks, and the quarrels and reconciliations of Louis XIV and La Vallière.[36]

Currito took Luis, and Luis let himself be taken, to the salon where the smartest society folk, the dandies, and the dudes of the village and the entire province had gathered. Out-standing among them was the Count of Genazahar, from the neighboring city of ———. He was an illustrious and re-spected figure. He had spent long periods of time in Madrid and Seville, and he patronized the best tailors, both for his regional clothes and his city attire. He had twice served in the Chamber of Deputies, and had made a complaint to the Gov-ernment concerning a chief magistrate who had overstepped his authority.

The Count of Genazahar was about thirty years old. He was good-looking, and knew it, and he made a boast of being

---

[35] *Mathilde was the sister of Richard the Lion-Hearted and Malek-Adel the brother of Saladin in a famous French novel of adventure and romance.*

[36] *Louis XIV, France's Roi Soleil, whose favorite mistress for many years was La Vallière.*

a man to be reckoned with in peace or war, duels or love affairs. Yet although he was one of the most persistent of Pepita's suitors, the Count had been rewarded with the gentle negative she was in the habit of giving to anyone who courted her and aspired to her hand.

The wound from that hard and bitter blow was still open in his conceited heart, it had not yet healed over. Love had turned to hate, and the Count often relieved his feelings by belittling Pepita.

He was engaged in this pleasant occupation when bad luck so willed it that Luis and Currito should arrive and mingle with the group of men listening to that bizarre eulogy. The crowd opened to receive them and Luis, as if the devil had so arranged it, found himself face to face with the Count, who was saying: "That Pepita Jiménez is not a bad actress. With more pretensions and more airs than the Infanta Micomicona[37] she tries to make us forget that she was born and lived in poverty until she married that scarecrow old enough to be her father, that damned usurer, and got her hands on his money. The only good thing that widow ever did in her whole life was to make a pact with Satan to hustle her knave of a husband off to hell, and rid the earth of so much corruption and so much pestilence. Now Pepita passes herself off as so virtuous and chaste. All good and well! God knows whether she's not carrying on with some rustic on the sly, making fun of everyone as if she were Queen Artemis." [38]

Quiet persons who never attend gatherings limited to men will be scandalized by such language. It will seem to them indecent and brutal beyond belief; but those who know the world will admit that such language is widely used, and that the prettiest ladies, the most amiable women, the most upright

---

[37] *An imaginary princess in* Don Quixote.
[38] *Greek counterpart of the Roman Diana, goddess of the chase.*

matrons are often the targets of language no less infamous and coarse, if they have an enemy, or even if they don't, for gossip, not to say defamation and scurrility, are often carried on as a pastime or witticism.

Since childhood Luis had never been accustomed to seeing anyone lose his sense of decorum in his presence, nor to hearing things said that might offend him, for during his childhood he had been surrounded by servants, relatives, and people who owed his father favors, and all of whom catered to him. Later at the Seminary, in part as the Dean's nephew, as well as because of his own merits, he had never been crossed, but had always been treated with consideration and flattery. Now he stood as though struck by a bolt of lightning as he heard the insolent Count drag the good name of the woman he loved through the dirt, defile it, and spatter it with filth.

Yet how could he defend her? To be sure, even though he was not Pepita's husband, or brother, or relative, he could take it upon himself to act as her champion; but he foresaw the scandal this would create when none of the laymen present arose to Pepita's defense and were all laughing at the Count's sally. Luis, being almost the minister of a God of peace, could hardly call the Count a liar and risk a quarrel with a man so devoid of shame.

He was on the point of holding his tongue and leaving; but his heart refused to sanction that. Making an effort to assume an authority that neither his youth, nor his face, more downy than bearded, nor his presence in that place could uphold, he began to speak with real eloquence against slanderers, and to upbraid the Count, sternly and with Christian candor, for the ugliness of his behavior.

His was a voice crying in the wilderness, or preaching in the desert. The Count answered his homily with wit and mockery; the crowd, including many outsiders, sided with the mocker, even though Luis was the son of the town's leading citizen. Even the worthless Currito, a paper tiger, failed to defend his friend, though he did not laugh, and Luis was forced to retreat under the weight of the ridicule, harassed and humiliated.

"That was all that was needed!" Luis muttered between his teeth when he reached home and returned to his room downcast and humiliated by the Count's jeers, which he exaggerated as he thought of them and which seemed to him unbearable. He flung himself into an armchair, depressed and discouraged, and a thousand conflicting ideas assailed his mind.

The blood of his father, boiling in his veins, awakened his wrath and urged him to cast off his clerical garb, as the villagers had advised him in the beginning, and to give the Count his just deserts. But instantly he was undone by the whole future he had laid out for himself, and he pictured the Dean denying him; likewise the Pope, who had already sent the pontifical dispensation that would permit him to be ordained before the required age, and the prelate of the diocese who had cited his proven virtue, learning, and the unwavering firmness of his vocation in his supporting petition for the dispensation. All of them appeared to accuse him.

He thought next to his father's jocular theory concerning the additives to persuasion resorted to by the Apostle James, the bishops of the Middle Ages, Ignatius Loyola, and other luminaries, and the theory no longer seemed to him so foolish. He was almost sorry he had not followed their example.

He recalled then the custom of an orthodox savant, an outstanding contemporary Persian philosopher, who had recently been mentioned in a book about that country. He would customarily punish the students and auditors with harsh words whenever they laughed during his lectures or failed to understand them. And if this did not suffice, he would step down from his chair, sabre in hand, and give them a sound drubbing. The method was efficacious, especially for settling an argument, though the philosopher had once or twice met an opponent of his own stamp, who had given him a tremendous slash across the face.

In the midst of his mortification and ill humor, Don Luis had to laugh at the memory of it. He felt sure that Spain was suffering no lack of philosophers who would gladly have adopted the Persian method; and if he himself failed to adopt it, it was certainly not through fear of being slashed, but from worthier and nobler considerations.

At last higher thoughts came to comfort his soul, and consoled him a little. "I did very wrong," he said to himself, "to preach a sermon in that place. I should have kept quiet. Our Lord Jesus Christ has said: 'Give not that which is holy unto the dogs, neither cast ye your pearls before swine, lest they trample them under their feet, and turn again and rend you.' [39]

"After all, what have I to complain of? Why should I return injury for injury? Why should I let myself be given over to wrath? Many holy Fathers have said: 'Anger in priests is even worse than lasciviousness.' The anger of priests has caused many tears to be shed, and has wrought much harm. Anger, an evil counsellor, has perhaps persuaded them that people need to sweat blood under divine pressure, and has brought before their angry eyes the vision of Isaiah. And they have seen and have made their fanatic followers see the gentle Lamb transformed into an inexorable avenger, descending from the peak of Edom, proud in the abundance of his strength, treading down nations as the vintner tramples the grapes in the wine-press, with his vestments lifted and drenched in blood to the thighs. Ah, no, my God! I am to be Thy minister. Thou

[39] *Matthew, VII, 6.*

art a God of peace, and my first virtue must be meekness. What Thy Son taught in the Sermon on the Mount must be my rule of conduct. Not an eye for an eye, a tooth for a tooth, but love thine enemy. Thou sheddest Thy light on the just and the unjust alike. Thou makest the blessed rain of Thy inexhaustible goodness to fall upon all. Thou art our Father, Who art in Heaven, and we should be perfect, as Thou art, forgiving those who offend us, and asking Him to forgive them for they know not what they do. I must remember the beatitudes. Blessed are ye when men shall revile you, and persecute you, and shall say all manner of evil against you falsely, for my sake.[40] The priest, he who is to become a priest, must be humble, peace-loving, pure in heart. Not like the oak, which stands proudly until the lightning strikes it, but like the fragrant herbs of the woods and the modest flowers of the field that yield their sweetest and most pleasant aroma when the peasant treads them down."

The hours passed in meditations of this nature until the clock struck three, and Don Pedro, just back from the country, entered his son's room to call him to dinner. The gay camaraderie of the father, his jests, his demonstrations of affection all failed to lure Luis from his melancholy or to give him an appetite. At the table he scarcely ate; he hardly spoke.

Don Pedro was deeply concerned over the mute sadness of his son, whose health, robust though it was, might be breaking down. However, Don Pedro rose at dawn and worked hard all morning, so after he had smoked a good Havana cigar with his coffee and had drunk a small glass of anisette, he went as usual to have his two- or three-hour siesta.

Luis took great care not to bring to his father's knowledge the offense he had suffered from the Count of Genazahar. His father, who was not a church-goer or patient by nature, would

---

[40] *Matthew, V, 11.*

instantly have set out to take the vengeance the son had not sought.

Finding himself alone, Luis left the dining room so as not to see anyone, and returned to the solitude of his room and sank still more deeply into his thoughts.

* * *

He had been buried in them for a long time, sitting in front of his desk with his elbows upon it, his right hand supporting his cheek, when he heard a sound nearby. He raised his eyes and saw beside him that busybody Antonoña. Bulky though she was, she had entered like a shadow, and was staring at him fixedly with a mixture of pity and anger.

Antonoña had taken advantage of the hour when the servants were eating and Don Pedro was sleeping to slip in without being seen by anyone; she had opened the door of the room and closed it behind her so softly that even if Luis had not been so absorbed, he would not have heard her.

Antonoña had come determined to hold a very serious conference with Luis, but she was not certain what she was going to say. She had prayed (whether to heaven or hell is not clear) for the gift of tongues so that she might speak less coarsely and clumsily than was her wont, and with the culture, elegance, and fitness needed for the noble reflections and fine feelings she considered it would be appropriate for her to express.

Upon seeing Antonoña, Luis frowned, showing clearly by his gesture how much that visit vexed him. He said in a brusque tone: "What have you come here for? Go away."

"I've come here to demand an accounting on behalf of my child," Antonoña replied, unperturbed, "and I'm not going to leave until I get it."

With those words, she drew a chair up to the writing desk and seated herself with aplomb and assurance across from Luis.

Seeing that there was no way out, Luis restrained his annoyance, armed himself with patience, and in a tone less cruel, he said, "Say what you have to say."

"What I have to say," Antonoña went on, "is that what you're doing to my little girl is wrong. You're behaving like a rascal. You've bewitched her. You've given her some evil potion. The little angel is going to die. She doesn't eat; she doesn't sleep; she can't rest, and it's all your fault. She's had two or three fainting spells today, just at the thought of your going. A fine kettle of fish you're leaving behind you before you're even ordained! Tell me, you wretch, why did you ever come here? Why didn't you stay with your uncle? She has fallen into your treacherous snares—she, so free, so much the mistress of her own will, captivating everyone and letting no one captivate her. No doubt that saintliness everyone was talking about was the lure you used. With your theology and your gibberish about heaven, you're like the heartless, wretched hunter who lures the stupid little thrushes into the net with a whistle."

"Leave me alone, Antonoña," Luis replied. "Stop tormenting me, for God's sake. I'm a wretch, I admit it. I should never have looked at your mistress. I should never have let her know that I love her; but I did love her, and I still love her, with all my heart. I never gave her any potion, nor philter; I gave her nothing but the true love I hold for her. All the same, it is necessary to wipe out, to forget this love. God has commanded me to do it. Do you suppose that the sacrifice I'm making is not immense, and will not always be? Pepita must gird herself with strength and make the same sacrifice."

"You don't even give the poor wretch that much comfort," Antonoña answered. "You voluntarily sacrifice on the altar that woman who loves you, who is yours, your victim. But where can she sacrifice you? What jewel has she, other than an ill-requited love, to throw out the window, what lovely piece of work to cast into the fire? How can she offer to God what she doesn't have? Is she to receive God and say to Him: 'My God, since he doesn't love me, here I am sacrificing him to You; I won't love him either'? God does not laugh; but if God did laugh, He'd laugh at such a gift."

Luis, utterly confused, did not know how to counter Antonoña's reasoning, which was worse than her earlier pinches. In any case, it was repugnant to him to discuss the metaphysics of love with that servant. "Let's lay aside these vain arguments," he said. "I cannot cure your mistress's illness. What can I do?"

"What can you do?" interrupted Antonoña, softer and actually affectionate now, her voice wheedling. "I'll tell you what you can do. If you can't cure my little girl's illness, you can at least relieve it. Aren't you supposed to be a saint? Well, the saints are both merciful and courageous. Don't run away like a coward and a boor, without saying good-bye to her. Come and see my little girl. She's sick. Perform this act of mercy."

"What can I accomplish with such a visit? I'd aggravate the illness instead of curing it."

"No you won't; you don't understand. You go there, and with that smooth talk and gift of gab that God gave you, you'll be able to drill some resignation into her head and leave her consoled. And if you tell her that you love her and you're leaving her only for God, at least her woman's vanity won't be trampled under foot."

"It would be tempting God to do what you're suggesting. It's dangerous for me and for her."

"And why should it be tempting God? If God sees the righteousness and purity of your intentions, won't He show

you His favor and His grace so you won't be lost on an occasion like this one I'm pointing out to you with so much justifica-
tion? Shouldn't you fly to liberate my little girl from her
despair and set her feet on the right path? If she should die
of sorrow at seeing herself rejected like that, or if, out of her
wits, she should grab a rope and hang herself from a beam,
believe me, your remorse would be worse than the brimstone
and sulphur flames from Lucifer's furnace."

"That would be awful! I don't want her to despair. I'll
gather all my courage and go and see her."

"Bless you! My heart told me you would! How good you
are!"

"When would you like me to go?"

"Tonight, on the stroke of ten. I'll be at the street door
waiting for you, and I'll take you to her."

"Does she know you've come to see me?"

"She doesn't know. It was all my own idea; but I'll prepare
her for your visit with great care so that the surprise, the unexpected delight, won't cause her to collapse in a faint. Will
you promise me you'll go?"

"I'll go."

"Good-bye. Now don't fail. At ten o'clock sharp. I'll be
at the door."

Antonoña ran out of the room, flew down the stairs two
at a time, and out into the street.

* * *

There is no denying that Antonoña proved most discreet
on this occasion. Even her language was so dignified and urbane
that some people might have doubts about everything that is
set down here, were it not corroborated by the best of evidence.
Moreover, we know full well what wonders the inborn clever-

ness of a woman can perform when personal interest or a *grande passion* are at stake.

Antonoña's affection for her little girl was undoubtedly great, and she could do no less than seek a remedy for her ills when she saw her so much in love and so desperate. The tryst to which she had just bound Luis was an unexpected triumph. So in order to turn that triumph to good account Antonoña had to arrange everything on the spur of the moment with profound worldly wisdom.

She had set the hour of the appointment for ten o'clock at night because this was the time of the now cancelled or suspended gathering when Luis and Pepita used to see each other. She chose it also to avoid gossip and scandal, for she had heard a preacher say that, according to the Gospel, nothing is so evil as scandal, and that the breeders of scandal ought to be flung into the sea with a millstone around their necks.

Antonoña went home to her mistress's house, well pleased with herself and firmly resolved to arrange things so skillfully that the remedy she had sought should not be useless, or even aggravate Pepita's illness instead of curing it.

She planned to give Pepita no warning other than to tell her at the last moment that Luis had of his own accord asked at what time he could pay her a farewell visit, and that she had set it for ten o'clock.

To avoid giving grounds for gossip, she planned not to let Luis be seen entering the house, and the hour and the arrangement of the house were very propitious to that purpose. The street would be full of people at ten o'clock owing to the fiesta, and Luis would therefore be noticed less as he walked along it. It would take him only a second to enter the vestibule where she would be waiting to lead him into the study without being seen by anyone.

Like most of the houses of wealthy Audalusian villagers,

Pepita's was more like two dwellings than one. Each house has its own door. Through the main door one enters the tiled patio with its arcades, the owner's living quarters and other rooms. The other door opens on the stable yard, stables, and coach house, kitchens, mill, wine-press, granaries, bins where the olives are stored before pressing; cellars where the oil, the new wine, the wine to be distilled, the brandy and vinegar are kept in huge jars; and wine vaults or storerooms where the good and aged wine is kept in casks or barrels. This second house, or section of a house, is called the country house, even though it may be in the middle of a town of twenty or twenty-five thousand people. The overseer, the foreman, the muleteer and the more important and permanent farm laborers in the master's service gather there at night, around the enormous fireplace in the great kitchen in winter-time, and in the open air or some cool, airy room in summer, resting and talking until their employers retire.

It seemed to Antonoña that the conversation and explanation she wanted her little girl and Don Luis to hold called for an atmosphere of calm, and no interruptions. Accordingly she decided that the girls who waited on Pepita were to be excused from all their duties and functions because that night was the eve of Saint John's Day, and should go to the country house to enjoy themselves. There they could make a night of it with the farm workers, doing the fandango to the click of castanets, singing and dancing to their hearts' content.

Thus the owner's house would be left empty and quiet, with no one there but herself and Pepita, with everything conducive to the solemnity, loftiness, and undisturbed calm needed for the interview she had prepared, and on which perhaps, or surely, depended the fate of two such estimable people.

* * *

While Antonoña was turning over in her mind and ar-
ranging all these things, Luis was no sooner alone than he began to repent of having acted so thoughtlessly and of agreeing
so weakly to the meeting Antonoña had requested.

He paused to consider Antonoña's rôle, and it seemed to
him more mischievous than Oenone's[41] or Celestina's.[42] He
could see before him all the dangers he had of his own accord
agreed to embark upon, but no advantage whatever in visiting
the lovely widow furtively and on the sly.

It seemed to him it would be disgraceful beyond words
for him to go and see her only to yield, to fall into her snares,
making light of his vows, flouting the Bishop who had recommended his petition for a dispensation, and even the Holy
Father who had granted it, and thus renounce the priesthood.
Moreover, it was a betrayal of his father who loved Pepita and
wanted to marry her. And to go and see her in order to shatter
her hopes completely struck him as a greater refinement of
cruelty than to leave without saying a word.

So reasoning, Luis's first impulse was to fail to keep the
appointment without any warning or excuse, leaving Antonoña
to wait for him in the vestibule in vain. But Antonoña might
already have announced his visit to her mistress, and failing
to go would be an unspeakable discourtesy not only to Antonoña but, above all, to Pepita.

Then he decided to write Pepita a most affectionate and
discreet letter, apologizing for not going, justifying his conduct, comforting her, showing his tender feelings for her, yet
making her see that duty and heaven must come before all else,

---

[41] *In Greek legend, the wife of Paris, who deserted her for Helen.
She refused to heal him, as she had promised she alone could do, when
he was wounded in the siege of Troy. In remorse for his death she
killed herself.*

[42] *Go-between in Fernando de Rojas' famous book* La Celestina, *who
was responsible for the tragedy of the young lovers Calixto and Melibea.*

and trying to give her the courage to make the same sacrifice as he.

Four or five times he set himself to write this letter. He scribbled one sheet after another, and tore each up, for the letter never came out to suit him. One time the letter came out dry, cold, pedantic, like a bad sermon or the droning of a dominie. The next, a puerile and unbecoming fear could be read between the lines, as if Pepita were a monster waiting to devour him. The next missive had other and no less deplorable defects. In short, after many sheets of paper had been used up in the attempt, in the end the letter was not written.

"I have no choice left," Luis said to himself. "The die is cast. Let's be brave and go."

He comforted himself with the hope that he would be quite self-controlled and that God would surely give him the gift of eloquence with which to persuade Pepita that she was a very good woman, that she herself had inspired him to fulfill his vocation, by sacrificing an earthly love and emulating the holy women who had denied themselves union not only with a sweetheart or lover, but even with their husbands, and had lived with them in matrimony as brother and sister, like Edward the Confessor, the English King, and his queen. After thinking this over, Luis felt more comforted and encouraged. He could see himself as King Edward, and Pepita as Queen Edith, his wife. And although resembling the queen in being virgin as well as wife, Pepita seemed to him far more genteel and poetic than the queen.

Nevertheless, Luis did not feel as sure and calm as he should after having made up his mind to imitate King Edward. He still found a certain something wrong about that visit he was going to make without his father's knowledge, and was on the verge of going and wakening him from his siesta and telling him everything. Two or three times he got up from his chair and started to go to his father; but each time he paused, thinking such an action beneath him, and shamefully childish. He felt free to reveal his own secrets, but to reveal those of Pepita in order to square himself with his father would be an ugly deed. He realized that it was the fear of lacking the strength to withstand her that motivated him, as well as the ridiculousness and baseness of such an action. Don Luis kept his peace, then, and said nothing to his father.

Moreover, having made that mysterious appointment, he did not even feel sufficiently at ease and sure of himself to approach his father. He had become so wrought up and beside himself from the opposing passions warring for possession of his soul that the room could not hold him: as though leaping or flying, he measured the length of his room in three or four strides, and even though it was large, he was in danger of bumping his head against the walls. And although the window was open, as it was summer, it seemed to him that he was about to smother; that the ceiling was weighing down his head; and that he needed all the air there was to breathe and all the limitless space there was to walk in; to lift his head and sigh and let his thoughts fly upward, he must have nothing above him but the vault of the sky.

Goaded by this need, he took his hat and stick and went out into the street. Once there, he avoided everyone he knew and sought solitude in the country, where he buried himself in the thickest and most remote part of the popular groves, gardens and paths which surround the village and make a paradise of its outskirts for more than half a league in all directions.

* * *

Until now we have said little about Luis's appearance. Be it known, then, that he was a good-looking young man, in the fullest sense of the word: tall, slender, and well-formed, with black hair and black eyes too, which were full of fire and sweetness. His dark skin, his white teeth, and his well-shaped, full lips gave him a haughty aspect; and in his whole bearing there was something dashing and manly in spite of his clerical reserve and meekness. And, finally, there was in his mien and air that unmistakable seal of distinction and nobility which would seem to be, though this is not always the case, the peculiar quality and exclusive privilege of aristocratic birth.

To look at Luis, one would have to confess that Pepita Jiménez responded instinctively to beauty.

Luis ran rather than walked along those paths, leaping brooks and scarcely noticing anything, like a bull stung by a gadfly. The farmers he met, the gardeners who saw him pass, perhaps took him for a madman.

Tired at length of moving aimlessly, he sat down at the foot of a stone cross, near the ruins of an ancient Paulist convent some three miles from the village. There he sank anew into meditation, but so confused that even he did not know what he was thinking.

The chiming of bells, summoning the faithful to prayer and reminding them of the Archangel's salutation to the Most Blessed Virgin came floating through the air to that retreat; they roused Luis from his ecstasy and brought him back to the world of reality.

The sun was just disappearing behind the lofty peaks of the nearby mountains, silhouetting the pyramids, pinnacles and broken obelisks of the summit against a background of purple and topaz as the setting sun turned the sky to gold. The shadows began to lengthen across the plains, and the tallest crags of the mountains opposite those behind which the sun was going down gleamed like red-hot gold or crystal.

The windowpanes and the white walls of the distant

sanctuary of the Virgin, the patroness of the village, crowning a hill, as well as another little temple or hermitage on another nearby hill called Calvary, still shone like two guiding beacons, touched by the last oblique rays of the dying sun.

Nature was filled with a melancholy poetry, and in the silent music the spirit alone can hear, all things seemed to be singing a hymn to the Creator. The slow pealing of the bells, muted and half lost in the distance, scarcely disturbed the earth's repose, and invited one to prayer without distracting the senses with sound. Luis took off his hat, knelt at the foot of the cross whose pedestal had served him as a seat, and said the Angelus with deep devotion.

The shadows were rapidly gaining ground; but as night unfolded and spread her cloak over those regions, she was pleased to adorn the sky with the brightest stars and a pure white moon. The blue of the heaven was not changed to blackness; although it darkened, it kept its blue. The air was so clear and subtle that thousands and thousands of stars could be seen glowing in the endless ether. The moon silvered the tops of the trees and was reflected in the current of the brooks, which looked like a luminous and transparent fluid where rainbows were made, changeable as the colors of an opal. The nightingales sang from the depths of the woods. The grasses and flowers exuded their generous perfume. Glow-worms without number gleamed like diamonds or rubies along the banks of the irrigation ditches among the thick grass and wild-flowers. There are no fireflies in that region, but glow-worms abounded, and shed a beautiful light. Many fruit trees still in blossom, many acacias, and countless rosebushes perfumed the air and filled it with a soft fragrance.

Luis felt overcome, seduced, overpowered by Nature's voluptuousness, and he doubted himself. Nevertheless, he was obligated to keep his pledged word and go to the appointment.

Taking the long way around, following other paths, vacillating at times whether to go to the source of the river, a delightful spot where the crystalline flow that irrigated the gardens sprang from the living rock at the foot of the mountains, Luis made his way toward town with slow and reluctant feet.

The nearer he came, the greater grew the terror he felt at what he had resolved to do. He crossed through the densest thickets, hoping to see some horrendous apparition, some sign, some warning to turn him back. He kept thinking of the student Lisardo, and he felt a strong desire to witness his own burial. But the heavens, smiling down with a thousand lights, moved all things to love. The stars were gazing lovingly at one another; the nightingales poured out their love songs; even the crickets were quivering their shrill-sounding wings amorously, like troubadours plucking the strings of their lute. The whole earth seemed given over to love on that tranquil and beautiful night. No signs, no portents, no funeral pomp; all was life, peace, and delight. Where was his Guardian Angel? Had it given Luis up for lost? Or was it not bothering to draw him back from his plan, having decided he was in no danger whatsoever? Who knows? Perhaps a triumph would come out of such perils. The example of King Edward and Queen Edith appeared once more to Luis's imagination and reinforced his will.

Carried away by such thoughts, Luis proceeded slowly, and was still some distance from the village when the church tower clock struck ten. The ten strokes were like ten blows falling upon his heart. They actually pained him, though the pain and fright were mixed with a treacherous eagerness and a tempting sweetness.

Luis hastened his step so as not to arrive too late, and soon found himself inside the village.

The town was very animated. The unmarried girls were trooping to the public fountain to wash their faces there and thus insure that the sweethearts of the girls who had them would be true, and that those who had none would find one. Here and there women and children were returning from gathering verbena, branches of rosemary, and other herbs for the making of magical potions. Guitars were strumming. The colloquies of love could be heard, and happy loving couples were to be seen on every hand. Though Saint John's is a Catholic feast, it retains certain vestiges of paganism and ancient nature-worship, perhaps because the feast practically coincides with the summer solstice. The fact is that it once was entirely secular, not religious. All was love and courtship. In our old ballads and legends, the Moor always abducts the beautiful Christian princess and the Christian knight always has his way with the Moorish princess on the eve and morning of Saint John, and the people might be said to cling to the tradition of the old ballads.

The streets were aswarm with all the villagers and the visitors. Passage was made difficult by the number of fruit stands, doll and toy booths, small counters holding almond cakes, spice cakes, and roast peas, and bun booths where gypsy women, young and old, were frying the batter, making the air reek with the smell of cooking oil. They weighed and served the pastries; they replied wittily to the flattery of the passing young men, or told people's fortunes.

Luis was trying to avoid his friends. If he saw one of them in the distance, he crossed to the other side of the street. Thus he gradually approached the vestibule of Pepita's house without being spoken to or detained. His heart began to pound violently and he paused a moment to get himself in hand. He looked at his watch; it was close to ten-thirty.

"Good Heavens! She has been waiting for me nearly half an hour!"

He rushed forward and entered the vestibule. The lantern that always lighted it was dim that night.

Luis had no more than entered the vestibule when a hand, a talon rather, seized him by the right arm. It was Antoñona and she said to him in a low voice: "You devil of a seminarian, you ingrate, you dolt, you idiot! I was thinking you weren't coming. Where have you been, good-for-nothing? How dare you be late, how dare you hold back on me when the salt of the earth is melting for you, and the sunlight of beauty is waiting?"

Antoñona did not stand still as she voiced those complaints, but walked ahead, dragging the silent and confused seminarian after her, still clutched by the arm. They passed through the grilled gate separating house and yard, and Antoñona closed it quickly without a sound. They crossed the patio, climbed the stairs, passed through several corridors and two rooms, and came to the door of the study, which was closed.

Perfect silence reigned throughout the house. The study was toward the rear where street noises could not reach it. All that could be heard, though blurred and faint, was the click of the castanets, the sound of guitars, and a light murmur, all coming from Pepita's servants who were holding their celebration in the country house.

Antoñona opened the office door, gave Luis a push and at the same time announced him, saying: "Child, here's Don Luis, who has come to say good-bye to you."

Having made the announcement with the proper formality, Antoñona discreetly withdrew from the room and closed the door, leaving the visitor and the girl facing each other.

* * *

At this point in the story we cannot fail to notice its ring of authenticity, and marvel at the scrupulous exactitude of the person who compiled it. For who can doubt that if there were anything contrived in these First and Second Chronicles, as in a novel, an interview as important and transcendent as this between Pepita and Luis would have been arranged through means less vulgar than those set forth herein? Perhaps our protagonists, while taking another country outing, would have been overtaken by a sudden and terrible storm, and would have had to take refuge in the ruins of some ancient castle or Moorish tower, indubitably rumored to be haunted by ghosts or something of the sort. Perhaps our hero and heroine would have fallen into the hands of a band of outlaws, from whom they would have escaped, thanks to the coolness and intrepidity of Luis, and then the two of them alone, having no other choice, would have taken shelter for the night in a cave or grotto. Or the author might perhaps have arranged things in such a way that Pepita and her yea-and-nay admirer would have had to take a sea voyage, and though there are no pirates or corsairs nowadays, it would not be difficult to invent a good shipwreck, in which Luis would save Pepita, and they would have been cast up on a desert island or some other poetic, far-off place. Any of these situations would have paved the way more artfully for the impassioned conversation of the young people, and would have put Luis in a better light.

We think, however, that, instead of criticizing the author for failing to avail himself of such complications, it would be better to thank him for his scrupulous conscience, and for sacrificing to the fidelity of the story the impact he might have made had he ventured to embellish and embroider it with situations and episodes drawn from his imagination.

Unless Antonoña's ingenuity and officiousness and Luis's weakness in promising to keep the engagement were the actual

reality, why should the author invent fictions and arrange for
them to see and speak to each other at the greatest peril to the
virtue and integrity of both? There was no need for that.
Whether Luis behaved well or badly in coming to the appointment, and whether Pepita Jiménez, who had already been told
by Antoñona that Luis was coming of his own accord to see
her, did right or wrong in rejoicing at his somewhat mysterious
and untimely visit, let us not blame it all on chance, but rather
on the persons who figure in this story themselves, and the
passions that move them.

We are very fond of Pepita; but the truth must prevail,
and we must speak it even though it be prejudicial to our
heroine. Antoñona had told her at eight o'clock that Luis was
coming, and Pepita, who had been talking about dying, whose
eyes were red, her eyelids inflamed from crying, and her hair
dishevelled, from that moment could think of nothing but how
to make herself ready to receive Luis. She washed her face
with warm water to take away the tear-stains, but only to the
point where they no longer looked ugly, not to do away with
the evidence that she had been crying. She dressed her hair
in such a way as to show a certain artistic and genteel carelessness, though not an indecorous disorder, rather than a studied
arrangement. She polished her fingernails and put on a simple
house dress, as it would not be proper to receive Luis in a
dressing-gown. In a word, she instinctively saw to it that all
the details of her toilet combined to make her look her most
charming and neat, without showing the slightest trace of the
care, effort and time employed, as though everything were the
work of nature, an inherent gift, something that persisted, as it
were, in spite of the neglect of her person caused by the vehemence of her affections.

As we came to learn, Pepita spent more than an hour on

these labors at her dressing table, which were to manifest themselves only by their effect. Then she put on the finishing
touches and glanced into the mirror with ill-disguised satisfaction. Finally, at about nine-thirty, she picked up a candlestick and went down to the room where the Infant Jesus was
enshrined. She first lighted the burned-out candles on the little
altar; she felt a twinge of conscience as she looked at the
withered flowers; she asked the forgiveness of the holy image
for having neglected it so long; then, falling to her knees, she
prayed with all her heart and with the confidence and trust
inspired by One who has dwelt in the house for many years.
Pepita would not have ventured to ask of an image of the
Nazarene crowned with thorns and carrying his cross; of an
Ecce-Homo, rejected and scourged, holding a reed as a derisive
scepter, His hands bound with a rough cord; of a Christ
Crucified, bleeding and dying, what she could ask of her Jesus,
still a little child, smiling, beautiful, healthy, and fresh-colored.
She begged Him to leave her Luis; not to take him away; for
He, so rich and well supplied with everything, could give up
that servant without undue sacrifice and yield him to her.

Having completed the preparations that might fairly be
classified and divided into cosmetics, attire, and religion, Pepita
settled herself in her study to await the coming of Luis with
feverish impatience.

Antonoña had been wise not to say he was coming until
shortly before the appointed hour. Even so, owing to the tardi-
ness of the young man, poor Pepita, full of anxiety and anguish,
was in a turmoil from the time she offered up her prayers and
pleas to the Child Jesus, until she saw the other child inside
her study.

* * *

The visit started off in a most serious and ceremonious style. The customary greetings were spoken mechanically on both sides. Luis, when asked to sit down, took an armchair without laying aside his hat and stick, and at a safe distance from Pepita, who was seated on the sofa. A lamp table stood beside her, holding books and a candlestick that lighted up her face. A lamp was also burning on the desk. The room was so large that even with the two lights most of it was left in shadow. A large window overlooking a small inner garden was open because of the heat, and although the iron grating was like the weft of a tapestry of climbing roses and jasmine, the bright rays of the moon found a path through the foliage and the flowers, entered the room, and competed with the lamp and candle. The distant and confused sounds of the merriment in the country house on the other side, also entered through the open window, mingling with the monotonous murmur of a fountain in the little garden. The scent of the jasmine and roses covering the window blended with that of the campanula, sweet basil, and other plants that adorned the beds beneath it.

A long pause ensued, a silence as difficult to maintain as to break. Neither of the two ventured to speak. The situation was, in fact, highly embarrassing. It was as arduous a task for them to express themselves then as for us to report now what they had to say; yet we have no choice but to undertake it. Let us permit them to speak for themselves and transmit their words verbatim.

"At last you've deigned to come and say good-bye to me before your departure," said Pepita. "I had given up hope."

The rôle that Luis was playing was a difficult one, and it must be borne in mind that even men no longer neophytes, but experienced and adroit in these dialogues, often fall into foolishness at the start. Do not condemn Luis, then, if in the beginning he talked nonsense.

"Your complaint is hardly fair," he said. "I came here with my father so say good-bye to you, and as we hadn't the pleasure of being received by you, we left our cards. They told us you were somewhat indisposed, and every day we have sent to learn how you were. Our satisfaction was great when we learned that you felt better. You are better now?"

"I could almost tell you I'm not better," Pepita replied. "But I see that you're here as your father's emissary, and as I shouldn't like to make such an excellent friend feel badly, I feel bound to tell you I am considerably improved so that you may repeat it to your father. It's odd that you've come alone. Since Don Pedro didn't come with you, he must have had a great deal to do."

"My father didn't accompany me, señora, because he does not know I've come to see you. I've come alone because I mean my farewell to be solemn, serious, perhaps final, and his is of a very different nature. Father will come back here within a few weeks, but it's possible I may never return; and if I do return, it will be as one very different from what I am now."

Pepita could not restrain herself. The happy future she had been dreaming of vanished like a shadow. Her unshakable resolution to win that man at any cost, the only man she had ever loved in her life, the only one she felt capable of loving, had now become a futile resolve. Luis was leaving. All Pepita's youth, grace, beauty, and love were of no avail. Beautiful as she was, she was condemned to perpetual widowhood at the age of twenty, to solitude, to go on loving one who did not love her. Any other love would be impossible for her. Pepita's character was such that obstacles merely enhanced and stimulated her desires; a decision, once taken, assumed precedence over everything else until it had been carried out, and these qualities now manifested themselves with a vehemence that brooked no restraint. She would either get what she wanted or die in the attempt. The social considerations that are acquired in the great world, the deep-rooted custom of dissimulating and concealing the emotions, which place a ban on outbursts of passion, veil the most energetic explosion of poorly-repressed emotions, and dissipate them in ambiguous phrase and paraphrase, were meaningless to Pepita, who had had little knowledge of the world and knew no half-way measures. All she had known was blind obedience to her mother and her first husband, and later to demand that same obedience of all other human beings. Accordingly, when Pepita spoke on that occasion she revealed herself for what she was. Her impassioned nature was apparent in her words, and her words served to define rather than dissimulate her thoughts and her feelings. She spoke not as a lady from our salons would have spoken, with certain circumlocutions and attenuations in her expression, but with the idyllic forthrightness that Chloe had used in speaking to Daphnis,[43] and with the humility and complete yielding of Naomi's[44] daughter-in-law offering herself to Boaz.

Pepita said: "You're going to persist in your plan, then? Are you certain of your vocation? Aren't you afraid of being a bad priest? Don Luis, I'm going to forget for the moment that I'm an untutored girl; I'm going to lay aside all my feelings; and I'm going to argue coldly, as if the subject under discussion had nothing to do with me. Here are the facts, which can be interpreted in two ways, and either way, you come out badly. Let me say what I have to say. If a woman, certainly not very forward in her coquetries, has succeeded in interesting you within a few days of your seeing her and meeting her, with barely a word to you; if she can move you to look at her

---

[43] *Daphnis, a goatherd, and Chloe, a shepherdess, were the protagonists of a Greek romance of idyllic love.*

[44] *In the Bible Ruth, the daughter-in-law of Naomi, remained faithful to her, even after her husband's death. She later married Boaz, a kinsman of Naomi.*

with a glance that augurs profane love, and has even succeeded in arousing you to a demonstration of affection, which is a lapse, a sin in anyone, and how much more so in a priest; if this woman is, as indeed she is, a villager, commonplace, uneducated, without talent, without distinction, what can you expect in the big cities when you will have to see, meet and visit other women a thousand times more dangerous? You'll lose your head when you see and meet the great ladies who live in palaces, who walk on soft carpets, who glitter with diamonds and pearls, who wear silks and laces in place of percale and muslin, who bare their white, well-turned throats, instead of covering them with a modest, plebeian kerchief. Those women are more skilled in wounding with a glance; the very ostentation, publicity, and pomp that surround them, make them seem the more desirable for being apparently inaccessible; they can discuss politics, philosophy, religion, and literature; they can sing like canaries, and seem wrapped in clouds of perfume, adoration, and surrender, placed upon a pedestal of triumphs and victories, deified by the prestige of an illustrious name, exalted in gilded salons, or withdrawn to voluptuous boudoirs where only the fortunate of the earth may enter; titled perhaps, called Pepita, Antonita, or Angelita only by their intimates, and by the rest of the world Her Grace, the Duchess or the Marchioness. If you have succumbed with every sign of enthusiasm to a rustic villager on the eve of being ordained, and if you have yielded to a fleeting infatuation, am I not right in foreseeing that you're going to make a wretched priest, unchaste, worldly, and a misfit, and that you'll surrender at every turn? Don't be offended with me for this theory, Don Luis, but believe me, you would be worthless even as the husband of a chaste woman. If you have clasped a woman's hands with the eagerness and tenderness of an impassioned lover, if you've sent looks that promised heaven, an eternity of love, and if you have . . . kissed that woman, who aroused in you nothing but what I shall leave nameless, then go with God, and don't marry her. If she is a good woman, she will not want you for a husband, nor even for a lover; but, for the love of God, don't become a priest either. The Church needs different men, more serious and more capable of virtue, as ministers of the All Highest. But if, on the contrary, you have felt a great love for that woman we're talking about, though she may scarcely be worthy of it, why abandon her and deceive her cruelly? If she has inspired in you that grand passion, however unworthy she may be, don't you think she shares it and will be its victim? Tell me, when love is great, lofty, and strong, does it ever fail to triumph? Doesn't it dominate and irresistibly subjugate the beloved object? By the quality and the purity of your own love you should measure that of your beloved. And how can you not fear for her if you abandon her? Has she the manly energy, the persistence that leads to the knowledge contained in books, the stimulus to seek fame, the multiplicity of grandiose plans, and all the rest in your cultivated and sublime mind that can serve to distract and separate you from all other earthly affection without shattering violence? Don't you understand that she will die of grief, and that you, destined to make the bloodless sacrifice on the altar, will begin by ruthlessly sacrificing the one who loves you most?"

"Señora," Luis replied with an effort to conceal his emotion and not to reveal by his tremulous and stammering voice how upset he was, "señora, I, too, have to control myself to answer you with the coldness of one who answers argument by argument, as in a controversy. But your accusation is so well-reasoned and—forgive me for saying it—so clever and sophisticated that I am forced to rebut it by reason. I wouldn't have thought I would be forced to hold forth here and to sharpen my poor wits; but unless I am to pass for a monster, you've forced me to do so. I will give you a full and complete reply to the dilemma on whose horns you have sought to impale me. Although I was reared in the Seminary at my uncle's side, where I did not see women, do not think me so ignorant nor so wanting in imagination that I never envisaged them in all their beauty, all their seductiveness. On the contrary, my imagination has gone beyond the reality. Called into being by the biblical songs and the secular poets I've read, women have appeared to me in fancy more elegant, more graceful, more discreet than those commonly to be found in the actual world. I realized it then, and even exaggerated the price of the sacrifice I was making in renouncing the love of such women and planning to raise myself to the dignity of the priesthood. I knew full well the charm it can and must add to a beautiful woman to dress her in rich fabrics and glittering jewels, to surround her with all the graces of the most refined culture and all the riches that the hand and the tireless mind of man can create. I knew very well, too, how much contact with the most notable men of learning, the reading of good books can polish, heighten, and add lustre to the intelligence of a woman, how much her natural gifts are enhanced by the atmosphere of flourishing cities and the monuments and grandeur they have to offer. I've pictured all this to myself so vividly and read of it all with such enchantment that, if I should come to meet and know such women as you mention, you need have no doubt that far from falling down in the adoration and madness you predict, I would perhaps suffer the disenchantment of realizing how far from the dream the reality would be, the difference between the model and the painting."

"Now those really are sophistries!" Pepita interrupted. "How can you deny that what the imagination paints is more beautiful than what actually exists? But how can you deny, either, that reality has more seductive power than what is imagined and dreamed? The vagueness and airiness of a phantom, however beautiful it may be, cannot compete with what materially arouses the senses. I can understand that religious images might conquer worldly dreams in your soul; but I'm afraid that religious images would not conquer worldly reality."

"You need have no fear, señora," Luis replied. "My imagination is more effective in what it creates than the entire universe is, in what comes to me through my senses—except for you."

"Why except for me? That arouses another suspicion in me. Can the idea you hold of me, the idea that you love, perhaps a creation of that powerful fantasy of yours, be an illusion that in no way resembles me?"

"No, no, it isn't. I'm convinced that this idea corresponds to you in every way; but perhaps it's innate in my soul. Perhaps it's been there since God created me; perhaps it's a part of the essence of my soul. Perhaps it's the purest and the richest part of my soul's self, like the perfume of flowers."

"I was right to be afraid! You're proving that now. You don't love me. What you love is the essence, the aroma, the purest thing in your soul, which has assumed a form similar to mine."

"No, Pepita; don't amuse yourself by tormenting me. What I love is you—you as you are. But this that I love is so lovely, so pure, so delicate that I cannot understand how it could have filtered through my gross senses and so have reached my mind. I suppose, I believe, and I am certain that it must have been in me already. It's like the idea of God, which was in me, which has developed and been magnified in me, but which has, nevertheless, a real object that is higher, infinitely superior to the idea itself. As I believe that God exists, I believe that you exist, and that you're worth a thousand times more than the idea I've formed of you."

"I still have a doubt left. Couldn't it be woman in general who has awakened this idea, and not I alone and exclusively?"

"No, Pepita. The magic, the sorcery of a woman, beautiful of soul and winning of person, had entered my imagination before I ever saw you. No duchess or marchioness in Madrid, no empress in the world, no queen nor princess on the whole earth is worth as much to me as the ideal and imaginary beings I've lived with. They appeared to me in palaces and boudoirs, magnificent in elegance, taste, and exquisite adornment, which I built in my imagination, ever since I reached adolescence, and which housed my Lauras,[45] Beatrices, Juliets, Marguerites and Eleanors, or my Cynthias, Gliceras, and Lesbias. I have crowned them in my mind with diadems and oriental miters, and wrapped them in cloaks of purple and gold, surrounded them with regal pomp, like Esther and Vashti.[46] I lent them the bucolic simplicity of the patriarchal age, like Rebecca and the Shulamite; I gave them the sweet humility and devotion of Ruth; I listened to them talk like the mistresses of eloquence, Aspasia or Hypatia. I enthroned them in marble halls and endowed them with the glory of noble blood and illustrious lineage, as if they were the proudest of the patrician matrons of Ancient Rome. I've pictured them as frivolous, coquettish, gay, full of aristocratic forwardness, like the ladies of the time of Louis XIV at Versailles, and I've dressed them sometimes in modest surplices that awakened veneration and respect, other times in tunics and fine-woven peplums through whose airy

---

[45] *Laura, the beloved of Petrarch; Beatrice, Dante's love; Juliet, Romeo's love; Marguerite, probably Margaret of Navarre, author of* The Heptameron; *Eleanor, probably of Aquitaine, wife of Henry II of England; Cynthia, surname of the goddess Diana; Lesbia, the Greek poetess Sappho.*

[46] *Vashti was the queen of Ahasuerus, King of the Medes and the Persians. For refusing to appear when he summoned her, he put her aside, and married the Jewess, Esther.*

folds all the supple perfection of their lovely forms was out-
lined, as well as in the transparent *coa* of the beautiful courte-
sans of Athens and Corinth, so that the white and rose of their
well-modeled bodies shone through the diaphanous material.
But, what price the delights of the senses, what price all the
glory and magnificence of the world, when a soul hungers and
thirsts for divine love, as I believed, perhaps with too much
pride, that mine hungered and thirsted? Great cliffs, entire
mountain ranges must yield if they present an obstacle to the
outburst of fire suddenly flaming in the breast of the earth,
must give way before the blasting powder of the mine and the
lava of a volcano in thunderous eruption. Even so, or perhaps
with more force, had my spirit cast aside all the weight of the
universe, all the created beauty which rested upon it, imprison-
ing it, hampering its flight to God, its center. No, no, I have
not rejected any gift through ignorance, nor any sweetness, nor
any glory. I recognized it all for even more than it was actually
worth when I cast it aside for another gift, another glory, another and greater sweetness. The profane love of woman has
come to me not only in imagination, with all the seduction it
holds, but with the sovereign and almost irresistible enchantment of the most dangerous of temptations, what the moralists
call the temptation of a virgin at a time when the mind, not
yet disillusioned by experience and sin, pictures in the love
embrace a supreme delight, doubtless immensely greater than
any reality or any truth. As long as I've lived, ever since I became a man, which is years ago now, for I am not so young,
I've despised all those shadows and reflections of beauty and
delight, because I was in love with an archetype of beauty,
thirsting for a supreme delight. I have striven to die within
myself in order to live in the beloved object; to strip not only
my senses, but even the powers of my soul bare of worldly
affections, of figures, of images, in order to be able to say with

truth that the living I is not I but Christ who lives in me. Perhaps I've committed sins through arrogance and over-confidence—surely I have—and God has decided to punish me. Then you crossed my path and led me astray, and I have lost my way. Now you upbraid me, you make fun of me, you accuse me of frivolity, and of being easily led; and when you upbraid me and make fun of me, you're offending your own self in supposing that my weakness could have caused me to succumb to any woman whosoever she might be. I don't want to commit the sin of pride when I should be humble by defending myself. If God has withdrawn His grace from me in punishment of my pride, it is more than possible that I have been made to waver and fall through the basest motives. I tell you, however, that my mind, perhaps deluded, understands it in quite another way. That may be the result of my unruly pride, but I repeat that I understand it in another way. I cannot bring myself to believe that there is baseness or villainy in the reason for my downfall. The reality I've seen in you has come to supersede and override all the dreams of my youthful imagination. You stand out above all the nymphs, queens, and goddesses. Above all my ideal creations, overthrown, broken, and undone by divine love, there arose in my soul the faithful image, the perfect copy of the living beauty that adorns, that is the essence of your body and soul. Something mysterious, supernatural even, may have played a part in this, for I loved you from the moment I saw you, almost before I saw you. Long before I knew that I loved you, I loved you. It is as though there were something foreordained in this; that it was written; that it was predestined."

"If it was written, if it was predestined," Pepita interrupted, "why not yield to it, why keep on resisting it? Sacrifice your plans to our love. Haven't I already sacrificed a great deal? Even now, am I not sacrificing my pride, my dignity, and my modesty in begging you, in striving to conquer your disdain? I believe I, too, loved you before I saw you. Now I love you with all my heart, and there can be no happiness for me without you. It is true that you will find no adversaries in my humble intelligence as powerful as I have in yours. Neither with my mind, my will or my love can I succeed in elevating myself to God at once. Neither by nature can I rise, nor even venture too long to rise to such lofty spheres. Yet my soul is filled with piety, and I know and love and adore God; but I can see His omnipotence and admire His goodness only through His handiwork. Even in imagination I cannot succeed in forging those dreams you mention. Nevertheless, I have dreamed that someone handsomer, more perceptive, poetic, and complete than the men who have courted me until now might love me, and that with a lover more distinguished and able than all my admirers in this village and those nearby, I might fall in love and surrender my will to him. That someone was you. I had a presentiment of it when they told me you had come to the village; I recognized it when I saw you for the first time. But as my imagination is so feeble, the picture I had formed of you came nowhere near what you are. I, too, have read some stories and some poetry, but out of all the elements I could remember of them I never succeeded in composing a picture that was not far inferior in merit to what I saw in you, and recognized in you from the moment I met you. And so, from the first day, I have been undone, and conquered, and destroyed. If love is what you say it is, if it means to die in one's self in order to live in the beloved, then my love is true and real, for I've died in myself, and I live in you and for you. I've longed to cast this love from me, thinking it ill-requited, but that was not possible. I've begged God with great fervor to take this love from me or to kill me, and God has not chosen to hear me. I've prayed to the Blessed Mary to wipe the image of you from

my heart, and my prayer has gone unheeded. I've made vows
to my name saint not to think of you, except as he thought of
his blessed spouse, but the saint has not come to my aid. In
view of all this, I've had the audacity to pray heaven that you
might let yourself be won over, and that you might lay aside
your plan to become a priest, that there might be born in your
heart a love as deep as that in mine. Luis, tell me frankly, has
heaven been deaf to this appeal, too? Or is it perhaps that a
small love suffices to overpower and conquer a small, unhappy,
weak soul like mine, whereas a more powerful love, which I
am not worthy to inspire, or not capable of sharing, perhaps
not even of understanding, is needed to subjugate your soul,
over which such lofty and powerful thoughts keep vigil and
custody?"

"Pepita," Luis replied, "it's not that your soul is smaller
than mine, but that it is free of obligations, whereas mine is
not. The love you've inspired in me is immense; but my obliga-
tion, my vows, the plans for my whole life, now on the point
of realization, are fighting against it. Why can't I say so without fear of offending you? If you achieve your love in me, you
are not humiliated. But if I yield to your love, I am humiliated
and diminished. I leave the Creator for His creature. I destroy
the work of my abiding choice, I break the image of Christ in
my breast, and the new man I've made of myself at such a
cost will vanish and the former man be reborn. Why, instead
of my descending to the earth, to these times, to the impurities
of this world, which I formerly disdained, don't you raise yourself to me by virtue of that very love you hold for me, cleansing
it of all dross? Why cannot we love each other without shame
and without sin or stain? God enters saintly souls with the pure
and refulgent fire of His love. He fills them in such manner
that they are replete with God, and in all are God, penetrated
throughout with God by the grace of divine love, like a metal

that comes from the forge all shining and glowing, all fire, yet
not ceasing to be metal. Such souls love one another and enjoy
one another, as if they were loving and enjoying God, loving
Him and enjoying Him because they are God. Let us rise,
together in spirit, let us climb this difficult and mystical ladder;
let us ascend together in spirit to this blessedness, which is possible even in mortal life. But to do so, we must be separate in
body; I must go where my duty, my promise, and the voice of
the All Highest call me, for I am His servant, destined to
worship at His altars."

"Ah, Don Luis," Pepita replied, all desolate and remorse-
ful, "I realize now how base is the metal from which I am
forged, and how unworthy to be entered and transformed by
divine fire. I shall tell everything, and cast aside even shame.
I'm a vile sinner. My gross and untutored spirit cannot grasp
those subtleties, those distinctions, those refinements of love.
My rebellious will rejects what you propose. I cannot even
conceive of you without you. To me you are your mouth, your
eyes, your black hair, which I long to caress with my hands;
your sweet voice and the charming tone of your words that
wound and truly enchant my ears—your whole corporeal form
in short, which seduces me and fills me with love, and through
which, and only through which, the invisible, vague, and
mysterious spirit reveals itself to me. My stubborn soul, incapable of such marvelous ecstasies, will never be able to follow you to the regions where you want to take it. If you succeed in raising yourself to them, I shall be left alone, abandoned, sunk in deepest affliction. I'd rather be dead. I deserve
to die; I desire it. Perhaps in dying my soul will loosen or
break infamous chains that hold it back, and become capable
of that love you want us to feel for each other. Kill me then;
kill me first so we can love each other like that, and my freed
spirit will follow you throughout space and will wander invisible beside you, watching over your sleep, raptly contemplat-

ing you, entering your most hidden thoughts, seeing your soul as it really is, without the intervention of the senses. But while I am alive this cannot be. I love you, not with my soul alone, but with my body, and I love the shadow of your body, and the reflection of your body in the mirror, and in the water, and your name and your surname, and your blood and everything that makes you Luis de Vargas—the timbre of your voice, your gesture, the way you walk, and I don't know what all else. I say again you must kill me. Kill me without mercy. No; I'm not a Christian; I'm a materialistic idolator."

Here Pepita came to a long pause. Luis did not know what to say, and was silent. Tears were running down Pepita's cheeks, and she went on, with a sob: "I know you despise me, and you do right to despise me. You'll kill me with that disdain I deserve more surely than with a dagger, without staining your hands or your conscience with my blood. Good-bye. I'm going to rid you of my hateful presence. Good-bye, forever."

With those words, Pepita rose from her chair, and without again turning her tear-stained face, beside herself, she rushed toward the door to the inner rooms. Luis felt an overwhelming tenderness, a fatal pity. He was afraid that Pepita would actually die. He followed her intending to stop her, but was not in time. Pepita went through the door, her figure was swallowed up in darkness. At though drawn by a superhuman power, impelled by an invisible hand, Luis entered the dark room behind Pepita.

* * *

The study was left empty.

The servants' dance must have been over, for there was not the least sound. Only the fountain in the little garden broke the silence.

No breath of wind disturbed the quiet of the night and

the serenity of the air. Through the window came the perfume of the flowers and the glow of the moon.

After a long time, Luis appeared again, out of the darkness. Terror was painted on his face, something like the despair of Judas.

He let himself fall into a chair and putting his elbows on his knees, he pressed his closed fists to his face; he stayed in that position for more than half an hour, doubtless sunk in a sea of bitter reflections.

Anyone seeing him would have suspected he had just murdered Pepita.

Pepita appeared later, however, slowly and with an air of deep melancholy she drew near where Luis was sitting, her face and eyes on the ground, and said: "Now I know, though too late, all the vileness of my heart and all the iniquity of my conduct. I have nothing to say in my defense, but I don't want you to think I'm more perverse than I really am. Please don't think there was trickery, or calculation, or plan to seduce you on my part. Indeed it was terribly wrong, but unpremeditated; a wrong perhaps inspired by the spirit of the devil that possesses me. Don't despair, don't torment yourself, for the love of God. You aren't responsible for any of it. A momentary madness, a delirium, took possession of your noble soul. Your sin is very slight. Mine is deadly, terrible, shameful. I deserve you less than ever now. Go; it's I who am now begging you to go. Go away, do penance. God will forgive you. Go, let a priest absolve you. Carry out your decision, and be a minister of the All Highest, cleansed anew of all wrong. You'll not only wipe out even the traces of this downfall by your hard-working and exemplary life, but, once you've forgiven me the evil I've done you, you will obtain Heaven's pardon for me. No tie binds you to me; and if there were, I hereby loosen or break it. You're free. I've done enough in having caused the morning star to fall unawares; I cannot, I must not, I would not keep it captive. Now you despise me more than you did; I sense it; I can infer it from your attitude; I see it. And you do right to despise me. There's no honor, no virtue, no shame in me."

As she said this, Pepita knelt and bowed down until her forehead touched the floor. Luis sat on in the same posture as before. For several minutes they both maintained a despairing silence.

Pepita finally went on in a choked voice, without raising her face: "Go now, Luis. Don't linger out of ignominious pity at the side of a woman like me. I will have the courage to suffer the aversion I've so merited, your forgetting me, and your contempt. I shall always be your slave, but far from you, far, far from you, so as not to bring back to your memory the infamy of this night." At the conclusion of her words, Pepita's voice was lost in her moans.

Luis could bear no more. He got to his feet, went to Pepita, and raised her in his arms, pressing her to his heart, gently pushing back the blonde curls that fell in disorder over her face, and covering it with passionate kisses.

"My darling," he finally said, "life of my soul, my heart's treasure, light of my eyes, raise your head, and prostrate yourself before me no longer. I am the weak-willed sinner, the wretch, the fool, the simpleton, not you. Angels and devils alike must be laughing at me and refusing to take me seriously. I've been a plaster saint, because from the beginning I've not been able to resist you and to free you from error, as I should rightly have done; and now I can't even manage to be a gentleman, a gallant and delicate lover who is duly grateful for his lady's favors. I don't understand what you saw in me to have fallen in love with me like this. There never was any solid virtue in me, nothing but the chaff and the pedantry of a schoolboy, who had read religious books as one reads novels, and had composed from them his own stupid novel about missions and contemplation. If there had been any solid virtue in me, I would have shown you your error in time, and neither of us would have sinned. True virtue doesn't fall so easily. In spite of all your beauty, in spite of your cleverness, in spite of your love for me, I would not have fallen if I had been really virtuous, if I had had a true vocation. God, who is all-powerful, would have lent me His grace. Undoubtedly something out of the ordinary, a miracle, would have been needed to resist your love; but if I had been worthy and if God had sufficient reason to do so, He would have performed the miracle. You do wrong in advising me to become a priest. I recognize my own unworthiness. Nothing but pride was motivating me. My ambition was a worldly one, like any other. What am I saying, like any other! It was worse; it was a hypocritical ambition, a sacrilege, simony."

"Don't judge yourself so harshly," Pepita replied, calmer now and smiling through her tears. "I don't want you to judge yourself like that, not even to find me not unworthy to be your companion. I want you to choose me out of love, freely, not to right a wrong, nor because you've fallen into the snare you may think I perfidiously set for you. Go, if you don't love me, if you are suspicious of me, if you don't esteem me. My lips will never utter a complaint if you abandon me forever and never think of me again."

Luis's reply cannot be fitted to the narrow and paltry loom of language. He broke the thread of Pepita's discourse by sealing her lips with his, and embracing her anew.

* * *

Some time later, with warning coughs and steps, Antonoña entered the study and said, "My, what a long conversation! The sermon this seminarian has been preaching was not the one of the seven words;[47] it's been almost the one of the forty hours.[48] It's time for you to go, Don Luis. It's nearly two o'clock in the morning."

"Very well," Pepita said, "he'll be leaving in a minute."

Antonoña again left the study and waited outside.

Pepita was transfigured. Joys she had never known in her childhood, pleasures and contentment she had never tasted during the years of her first youth, the lively activity and mischief that an austere mother and an old husband had curbed and dammed up in her until then, as it were, seemed now to burgeon suddenly in her heart as the green leaves of the trees burst their buds after the snows and ice of a long and severe winter have held them captive.

A city lady, familiar with what we call the social conventions, may find what I am about to say about Pepita strange and even deserving of censure; for, though innately well-bred, Pepita was a very natural creature, in whom feigned composure and all the circumspection practiced in the outside world had no place. Thus, with the obstacles that had stood in the way of her happiness overcome, and knowing that Luis had surrendered and promised of his own accord that he would make her his lawful wife, and rightly believing herself loved and adored by the man she loved and adored so much, she began to dance about and laugh and give other demonstrations of rejoicing in which there was much of childishness and innocence.

Luis had to leave. Pepita went for a comb and lovingly smoothed his hair, then kissed it. She straightened his tie.

"Good-bye, my beloved master," she said to him. "Good-

---

[47] *The seven words spoken by Christ on the Cross.*

[48] *The devotion called the "Forty Hours"—the exposition of the Sacrament for forty hours.*

bye, sweet king of my soul. I'll tell your father everything, if you don't want to. He's good, and he'll forgive us."

Finally the two lovers parted.

* * *

When Pepita was alone, her riotous gayety evaporated, and her face took on a grave and thoughtful expression.

She was considering two equally serious matters: the one of worldly interest, the other of a higher one. After the intoxication of love had faded, her first thought was that her conduct that night might lower her in Luis's opinion. But she made a stern examination of her conscience, and recognized that she had not acted through malice or premeditation in any way, and that what she had done was born of an irresistible love and of good impulses. Hence she believed that Luis could not ever despise her, and felt reassured on that point. Nevertheless, despite her candid confession that she could not comprehend a purely spiritual love, and even though her flight to the darkness of the bedroom had been an act arising from the most innocent of instincts, with no thought of consequences, Pepita could not deny to herself that she had later sinned against God, and on this point she could not excuse herself. She, therefor, commended herself to the Virgin, asking pardon with all her heart; she promised the image of the Virgin of Solitude, which stood in the convent, that she would buy seven handsome gold swords of delicate and ornate workmanship to adorn its breast; and she decided to go to confession to the Vicar on the following day and to subject herself to the harshest penance he could impose in order to win absolution for those sins, thanks to which she had overcome Luis's obstinacy. If not for them, he would certainly have become a priest.

While Pepita was turning all this over in her mind, and

handling the business of her soul with such skill, Luis had gone down to the vestibule, accompanied by Antonoña.

Before taking his leave, Luis said without preamble or circumlocution, "Antonoña, you know everything. Tell me who is the Count of Genazahar and what sort of relations he has had with your mistress."

"It hasn't taken you long to start being jealous."

"I'm not jealous; I'm only curious."

"So much the better. There's nothing more annoying than jealousy. Well, I'll satisfy your curiosity. The Count has just about run through his fortune. He's a rake, a gambler, and an addlepate. But he's prouder than Don Rodrigo[49] on the gallows. He took it into his head that my little girl must love and marry him, and now he's furious because she's turned him down a thousand times. But that hasn't stopped him from hanging on to more than a thousand dollars which Don Gumersindo lent him years ago without any security except a note. That was at Pepita's request, for she's got a heart of gold. So that fool of a Count must have thought that as Pepita had been kind enough to insist upon the loan when she was a married woman, she'd surely be kind enough, as a widow, to take him for a husband. Then came the awakening and the fury that followed."

"Good-bye, Antonoña," Luis said and went out into the street, now dark and silent.

The lights from the shops and the stalls of the fair had been extinguished, and people had gone to bed, except for the owners of the toy shops and other poor booth-keepers sleeping in the open air beside their merchandise.

Some persistent and tireless suitors still stood at the window grilles, talking with their sweethearts. Most of them had already disappeared, however.

In the street, out of Antonoña's sight, Luis gave free rein

---

[49] *Don Rodrigo Calderón, protégé of Phillip III of Spain.*

to his thoughts. His decision had been made, and a host of things came into his mind to confirm his resolution. The sincerity and ardor of the passion Pepita had inspired in him, her beauty, the youthful grace of her body and the springlike exuberance of her spirit arose in his imagination and filled him with happiness.

Yet Luis was reflecting with a kind of hurt vanity on the change in him. What would the Dean think? How shocked the Bishop would be! And most of all, wouldn't his father have very serious grounds for complaint? His displeasure, his anger when he should come to know of the engagement between Pepita and himself flashed into Luis's mind and worried him immeasurably.

As for what he had been calling his fall even before his downfall, he had to admit that now that he had fallen, it did not seem so very abysmal and appalling. Viewed in the new light he had just seen, he now judged his mysticism to have had no substance or consistency. It had been an artificial and empty product of his reading, of his boyish brashness, and the unfocused love of an innocent schoolboy. When he recalled that he had believed at times that he was receiving supernatural favors and gifts, had heard mystical whisperings, held interior dialogues, and almost begun to walk the unitive road of achieving inner prayer, which penetrates the soul to its depths and raises the intelligence to its apex, Luis had to smile at himself, and he suspected he had not been of entirely sound mind. It had all been his own presumption. He had never been a penitent, nor had he lived long years in contemplation. Never had he possessed sufficient merits to be favored by God with such lofty distinction. The most convincing proof to him of all this, the certainty that the supernatural gifts he had enjoyed had been sophistry, mere reflections from the authors he was reading, arose from the knowledge that none of all this had ever delighted his soul as much as Pepita's simple "I love you," or as her hand playing with his black curls.

Luis now had to resort to another kind of Christian humility to justify in his own eyes what he no longer wanted to call his downfall, but instead his change. He confessed to himself that he was not worthy to be a priest, and he now was prepared to look upon himself as a layman, a married man, a commonplace person, a good villager like any other, caring for his vineyards and olive groves, rearing the children he now wanted, and turning into a model husband at Pepita's side.

As this point, responsible as I am for the publication and disclosure of this story, I feel that it behooves me to interpolate various reflections and clarifications of my own.

I said in the beginning that I was inclined to believe that this narrative portion of the First and Second Chronicles was the work of the Dean, undertaken to complete the picture and to recount events not related in the letters. But at that time I had not yet read the manuscript carefully. Now, in view of the freedom with which certain matters are treated, and the author's broadmindedness toward certain lapses, I doubt that the Dean, whose rigidity I know on good authority, would have wasted his ink in writing what the reader has just read . . . Nevertheless, there is not sufficient reason to deny that the Dean may have been the author of the First and Second Chronicles.

The doubt remains, for when all is said and done there is nothing in the Chronicles that is opposed to Catholic doctrine or Christian morality. On the contrary, it will be seen upon careful examination that it conveys a lesson on the dangers of pride and arrogance, with special emphasis on the character of Don Luis. This story might easily serve as an appendix to the *Mystical Disenchanments* by Father Arbiol.

As for the position two or three prudent friends of mine

take—that if the Dean were the author, he would have related events differently, referring to Luis as "my nephew" and pointing a moral from time to time—I believe that those arguments carry little weight. The Dean set out to tell what happened, not to prove any thesis, and he did right to narrate it straightforwardly, and not to draw any morals. He was not wrong either, in my opinion, to conceal his personality and make no mention of himself, which goes to show not only his humility and modesty, but also his good literary taste, for epic poets and story-tellers who are worthy of serving as models do not use *I* when speaking of themselves, or even when they are the protagonists and actors in the events they are narrating. Xenophon the Athenian, to mention only one case, does not use *I* in the *Anabasis*,[50] but refers to himself in the third person whenever this is necessary, as if one man were doing the writing and another performing the deeds in question. Even so, there are a number of chapters in which Xenophon does not appear. Only shortly before the famous battle in which young Prince Cyrus was killed as he was reviewing the Greeks and barbarians who made up his army, despite the nearness of the army of his brother, Artaxerxes, which had been discerned from afar on the broad treeless plain, first as a small white cloud, then as a black spot, and finally, clearly and distinctly, with the neighing of the horses audible, the creaking of the war chariots armed with bellicose scythes, the trumpeting of the elephants, the music of martial instruments, and the glitter of the bronze and gold on their arms visible in the light of the sun, only at that moment, I say, and not before, did Xenophon appear to talk with Cyrus. He stepped out of the ranks to explain to him that the murmur spreading from Greek to Greek was nothing but what today we call the password, and which on that occasion was "Jupiter

---

[50] *The expedition of Cyrus against Artaxerxes and the retreat of the "ten thousand" Greeks described by Xenophon, a Greek historian.*

Savior and Victory." The Dean, a man of taste, well versed in the classics, was not likely to fall into the error of interjecting and intermingling himself in the story by virtue of being the hero's uncle and tutor, nor of boring the reader by popping out at every difficult and slippery pass with a "Look out," a "What are you doing?" a "Careful, don't fall, hapless man!" or some other warning of that nature. But not to have spoken up or remonstrated in some way, being present at least in spirit, was hardly fitting in certain of the episodes that have been recounted. For all these reasons, the Dean could therefore have written these First and Second Chronicles, with that great discretion which characterized him, but without countenancing what happened, as it were.

What he did do was to add glosses and edifying commentaries to such passages as called for them. But I have deleted them because annotated or glossed novels are out of vogue, and because if this little work carried the aforesaid additions, it would become somewhat voluminous.

As the one exception, and as a part of the text, however, I shall include at this point the Dean's note on the rapid transformation of Luis from mystic to non-mystic. The note is curious, and throws considerable light on the whole matter.

"This change in my nephew," he says, "did not surprise me. I had foreseen it from the time he wrote me the first letters. In the beginning, Luisito had misled me. I believed he had a real vocation, but later I realized that it was a vague poetic feeling. Mysticism was the vehicle of his poetry until a more adequate vehicle presented itself.

"God be praised that He willed Luisito's disenchantment in time! If Pepita Jiménez had not come to the rescue at the right moment, a fine priest he would have made! His impatience to achieve perfection in one bound should have put me on my guard if the affection of an uncle had not blinded me.

As though the favors of Heaven were to be obtained in an instant! One has only to arrive and triumph! A friend of mine, a sailor, told me that when he visited certain ports in America when he was young he would court the ladies with excessive haste, and they would say to him in their drawling American voices, 'You've just arrived and already you want to . . . Earn it, if you can!' If those ladies could say such a thing, what would Heaven say to the rash man who aims to gain it in the twinkling of an eye without deserving it? To begin to stand well with God and to enjoy His gifts, a man must strive hard; a great deal of purification is needed, a great deal of penance. Not even in the vain and false philosophies that have a touch of the mystical is there supernatural gift or favor without mighty effort and costly sacrifice. Iamblichus[51] lacked the power to evoke the genii of love and to call them forth from the fountain of Edgadara until after he had studied long and hard and mortified his body by privations and abstinence. Appolonius[52] of Tyana is supposed to have inflicted great physical punishment on himself before performing his false miracles. And in our day, the Krausists[53] who see God, actually see Him, or so they assure us, must read and learn the entire *Analytica* of Sanz del Río first, a most difficult undertaking that calls for more patience and suffering than would scourging the flesh until it is like a ripe fig. My nephew wanted to become a perfect man without turning a hand, and look where he landed! What matters now is that he should be a good husband, and that, since he was not made for great enterprises, he should be good at small and domestic ones, making that girl happy, for after all,

---

[51] *Fourth-century Syrian philosopher, leading exponent of Neo-Platonism.*

[52] *Greek philosopher, leading exponent of Neo-Pythagorism.*

[53] *Followers of Karl Christian Friedrich Krause, nineteenth-century German philosopher, who held that God is not a personality but an essence. Sanz del Río was his chief exponent in Spain.*

she was not to blame for anything except falling madly in love with him, with the candor and impetuousness of a savage."

So ends the Dean's annotation, written with unstudied frankness, as though to himself, for the poor man had no idea that I would play him the scurvy trick of having it published.

Let us now proceed with the story.

* * *

As we have said, in the middle of the street at two o'clock in the morning, Luis was mulling over the fact that his life, which up to that moment might be worthy of the Golden Legend, would now be changed into a sweet and perpetual idyll. He had been powerless to resist the snares of earthly love; he had not behaved at all like countless saints, Saint Vincent Ferrer among them, who had had to deal with a certain lascivious lady of Valencia. But the two cases were not comparable. If Saint Vincent's flight from that devil-possessed lady was an act of virtue, in Luis it would have been fleeing from the devotion, the innocence, and the meekness of Pepita, a thing as monstrous and heartless as if Boaz had given Ruth a kick and sent her on her way when she lay at his feet and said, "I am Ruth thine handmaid; spread therefore thy skirt over thine handmaid . . ." When Pepita surrendered to him, Luis was bound then to emulate Boaz and exclaim: "Blessed be thou of the Lord, my daughter, for thou hast showed more kindness in the latter end than at the beginning." In this way Luis excused himself for failing to imitate Saint Vincent and other saints less aloof. As for the ill success of his projected imitation of King Edward, he tried to put a good face on it and to excuse it. King Edward had married for reasons of State, because the nobles of the realm demanded it, though he felt no attraction to Queen Edith. But no reasons of State, no nobles great or small, had

figured in his and Pepita's case, only the most exquisite love
on both sides.

Be that as it may, Luis could not deny that he had destroyed his ideal, that he had been defeated, and this lent a
tinge of melancholy to his happiness. Those without ideals, or
who have never had one, would not take this to heart; but Luis
did. Accordingly, he thought of substituting a humbler and
more easily attained ideal for the old and lofty one. He recalled
that when Don Quijote was defeated by the Knight of the
White Moon, he decided to become a shepherd; and this recollection had an effect on him, for he intended, with the help
of Pepita Jiménez, to bring back to our prosaic and skeptical
age the happy age and the pious example of Philemon and
Bauchis,[54] by weaving an example of patriarchal life amidst
those pleasant fields, by founding in the village where he was
born a home all abrim with religion, which should be as well an
asylum for the needy, a cultural center, and a friendly gathering place, a shining mirror for other families. Finally they
would join conjugal love with the love of God, that God might
sanctify and visit their house, transforming it into a temple
where they would be both ministers and priests until heaven
should be disposed to carry them off together to a better life.

Two difficulties stood in the way of achieving this, difficulties that must first be removed, and Luis was prepared to
remove them. One was the displeasure, perhaps the anger of
his father, whom he had cheated of his fondest hopes. The
other was of a very different nature, and, in a way, more serious.

As long as Luis had planned to be a priest, it was not fitting for him to defend Pepita from the rude insults of the

---

[54] *In a story by Ovid, this poor Phrygian couple entertained Zeus so
hospitably that he promised to grant any request. They asked to die
together, and the god turned them into trees standing side by side.*

Count of Genazahar except by moral preachments. Nor could he wreak vengeance on those who had listened to his speech for their mockery and contempt. But once he had laid aside his clerical garb, and made ready to announce that Pepita was his betrothed whom he was soon to marry, despite his pacific character, his dreams of human loving-kindness and the religious beliefs still intact in his soul, which shrank from the thought of violence, Luis could not equate his dignity with forbearing to break the shameless Count's head. He knew full well that dueling was a barbarous custom; that Pepita had no need of the Count's blood to cleanse her of all stains of calumny and to rid herself of the Count. He even knew that the Count had voiced his insults because he was ill-bred and stupid, and not because, even in his deep resentment, he believed them. Nevertheless, Luis realized that in spite of all these considerations, he would never again be able to respect himself, he would never be able to play the role of Philemon successfully unless he began with that of Fierabras[55] by giving the Count his just deserts, while at the same time, praying to God that He never again confront him with such a choice.

Once his mind was made up to the deed, he decided to carry it out forthwith. It seemed to him ugly and absurd to send seconds and to permit Pepita's honor to be bandied about, and he therefore judged it more rational to seek a quarrel on some other pretext.

Furthermore, he supposed that in spite of the lateness of the hour the Count, an outsider and a confirmed gambler, might very well still be in the Casino, now turned into a gambling den. Luis went straight to the club.

It was still open, but most of the lights in the patio and the salons were out. Only one room was lighted. Luis made his

---

[55] *One of Charlemagne's paladins, noted for his size, who appears often in medieval romances.*

way toward it, and saw from the doorway that the Count of Genazahar was playing monte, with himself as croupier. Only five other people were playing. Two were outsiders like the Count; the other three were a cavalry captain in charge of remounts, Currito, and the doctor. Nothing could have suited Luis's purpose better. He watched them unseen, so absorbed were they in the game, then after a quick survey, left the club and went quickly to his house. A servant opened the door; Luis asked about his father and learned that he was asleep. Candle in hand, Luis climbed the stairs to his room on tiptoe so as not to be heard or to awaken his father. He put in his pocket about three thousand gold reales, which were his own money. He told the servant to unlock the door for him again, and returned to the club.

Stiff as a ramrod, as the phrase goes, Luis entered the salon where the men were playing, his steps ringing loudly. The players were astonished at seeing him.

"What are you doing here at this hour?" Currito asked.

"Where have you sprung from, little priest?" the doctor said.

"Are you going to preach me another sermon?" the Count cried.

"No sermons," Luis answered calmly. "The poor effect of the last one I preached has shown me beyond a doubt that God has not called me to that road, and I've chosen another. You've converted me, Count. I've laid aside my habit; I want to have some fun; I'm in the flower of my youth, and I want to enjoy it."

"Well, I'm glad," the Count interrupted. "But take care, boy, for if that flower is delicate, it can wither and shed its petals quickly."

"I'll watch out for that," Luis replied. "I see you're playing.

I feel lucky. You're dealing. Wouldn't it be a joke, Count, if I should win the bank from you?"

"You think it would be funny, eh? You've been eating too much red meat."

"I've been eating the kind of meat I like."

"This little popinjay is getting awfully quick on the comeback."

"I do whatever I like."

"Damn it all," said the Count. The storm was gathering, but the captain intervened and peace was completely restored.

"Come on," the Count said, calmed down and affable. "Get out your pennies and give your luck a whirl."

Luis sat down at the table and took all his gold out of his purse. The sight of it set the Count's mind at ease, for the amount was almost more than he had already in the bank, and he was anticipating the pleasure of cleaning out the novice.

"This game doesn't take much brains," Luis said. "I think I understand it already. I bet on a card, and if the card comes up, I win, and if the opposite happens, you win."

"That's the way it is, my young friend. You've got the mind of a male."

"Well, the best of it is that I have not only the mind of a male, but the will of a male, too. But withal, I'm not so much of a male in this company where there are already so many."

"You're full of talk and tricks."

Luis stopped talking. He played several hands and had such good luck that he won most of them.

The Count was beginning to feel worried. "Suppose the boy plucks me?" he said to himself. "Beginner's luck."

While the Count was growing anxious, Luis was feeling tired and irritated, and wanted to make an end of it at one stroke. "The object of all this," he said, "is to see if I can carry off that money, or whether you take mine. Isn't that right, Count?"

"That's right."

"Well, then, why should we stay here all night? It's getting late, and I ought to follow your advice and rest so the flower of my youth won't wither."

"What's that? You want to go? You want to quit while you're winning?"

"I don't care whether I win at all. Quite the contrary. Tell me, Curro, isn't there more in this pile of money here than in the bank?"

Currito looked and replied, "That's right."

"How shall I say it?" Luis asked. "I want to risk all there is in the bank on one card against an equal amount?"

"You can do that by saying '*copo*,' " Currito told him.

"*Copo*, then," said Luis, turning to the Count. "I'll bet all I have on the table and the game that the pair to this king of spades will turn up before my opponent pairs his three."

With all his available cash on the board, the Count was alarmed to see how he had been compromised; but he had no choice other than to accept the challenge.

The common saying is, "Lucky at cards, unlucky in love," but the more likely circumstances is that when good luck comes in one thing, it comes in everything, and the same thing is true of bad luck.

The Count kept drawing cards, but no three came up. He was very much upset, however hard he tried to dissemble. Finally he recognized the king of clubs and paused.

"Draw," the captain said.

"What's the use? The king of clubs! Damn it! The priestling has cleaned me out. Pick up the money."

The Count threw the deck furiously on the table.

Luis gathered in all the money with cool indifference.

After a brief silence, the Count said, "You'll have to give me a chance to make a comeback, priestling."

"I don't see why."

"It seems to me that among gentlemen . . ."

"By that rule, the game would never end," Luis observed. "By that rule it would be best to save oneself the trouble of playing."

"Give me another chance," the Count replied, without attempting to argue.

"All right," Luis said. "I want to be generous."

The Count picked up the deck and got ready to deal.

"Hold on a minute," Luis said. "Let's have an understanding first. Where's the money for the new bank?"

The Count was perturbed and confused. "I haven't any more money here," he answered. "It seems to me my word ought to be enough."

Luis said then in an even, quiet tone, "Count, I would have no objection to taking the word of a gentleman and becoming his creditor, if I were not afraid of losing his friendship, which I've almost gained now. But this morning I saw the cruelty with which you treated certain friends of mine, creditors of yours, and I should not want to find myself in the same position. It would be foolish for me voluntarily to incur your anger, as I would do if I lent you money, which you would not repay me, as you have not repaid Pepita Jiménez, except with insults."

The offense was all the greater for the fact that the charge was true. The Count turned livid with rage, and rising to his feet, impatient to come to blows with the seminarian, he said in a loud voice, "You lie, you foul-mouthed priestling! I'm going to tear you limb from limb with my own hands, you son of a . . ."

That final insult which reminded Luis of the stain on his

birth and besmirched the honor of the one whose memory was most dear and respected, was never completed, did not reach his ears.

Luis leaned across the table that stood between him and the Count, stretched out his right arm with startling speed, aim, and strength, and slashed his enemy across the face with the light cane he was carrying. The blow instantly raised a purple welt.

No defiance, no outcry, no disturbance followed. When the hands take over, tongues are stilled. The Count was ready to throw himself at Luis and destroy him if he could; but public opinion had made an about-face since morning and now favored Luis. The captain, the doctor, and even Currito, bolder now, held the Count, who struggled fiercely and tried to free himself. "Let me go, let me kill him," he said.

"I'm not trying to avert a duel," said the captain. "That is inevitable. I'm only trying to keep you from fighting here like a couple of louts. It would be an offense to my own decorum to stand by and watch it."

"Have some weapons brought," the Count said. "I don't want to delay the duel even one minute . . . Right now . . . here."

"Do you want to use sabers?" the captain said.

"That's all right with me," answered Luis.

"Fetch the sabers," the Count said.

They were all speaking in low voices so as not to be heard in the street. Even the servants of the club asleep on the chairs, in the kitchen, and in the patio, were not awakened.

Luis chose the captain and Currito as his seconds; the Count, the two strangers. The doctor stayed to do his duty and hoist the colors of the Red Cross.

It was still dark. They agreed to lock the doors and make the salon the dueling ground.

The captain went to his house for the sabers and a moment later he was back with them beneath the cloak he had put on to conceal them.

We know that Luis had never handled a weapon in his life. Luckily, even though the Count had never studied theology nor thought of becoming a priest, he was not much more dexterous as a fencer.

The conditions agreed upon for the duel were that once the two adversaries had sabers in their hands, they were at liberty to do whatever God should put into their heads.

The door to the room was locked.

The tables and chairs were moved back into a corner to clear the terrain. The lights were placed conveniently. Luis and the Count then took off their jackets and waistcoats and stood in their shirtsleeves as they picked up their weapons. The seconds stepped to one side. At a signal from the captain, the duel began.

The fight between two people who did not even know how to parry or defend themselves was bound to be very short, and indeed it was.

The Count's fury, which had been restrained for several minutes, exploded and blinded him. He was robust; he had a pair of iron fists, and let fly with a rain of disorderly random slashes. He touched Luis four times, fortunately always with the flat of the blade, and bruised his shoulders but did not wound him. It took all the young theologian's strength to keep from falling under the heavy blows and the pain of the contusions. The Count struck at Luis a fifth time and hit him a glancing blow on the left arm with the blade. Luis's blood began to flow copiously. But far from tempering his attack, the Count rushed at him again with even greater fury, and came almost under Luis's saber. Instead of trying to parry him, Luis brought his saber down briskly in a blow that opened a cut on the Count's head. The blood gushed forth, spread over his forehead and ran down into his eyes. Stunned by the blow, the Count fell full length to the floor.

The entire duel was a matter of a few seconds.

Luis had kept cool, like a Stoic philosopher forced into a conflict so at variance with his habits and trend of mind by the hard law of necessity. But no sooner did he see his opponent prostrate, covered with blood, and as if dead, than he felt such a keen dismay that he was afraid he might faint. He who had thought himself incapable of killing a sparrow had just come close to killing a man. He who only five or six hours earlier had still been resolved to become a priest, a missionary, a minister and messenger of the Gospel had committed, or accused himself of having committed, in no time at all every crime, and of having broken all the commandments of God's law. Not a mortal sin with which he had not contaminated himself. First his plans of heroic and perfect sainthood had faded. Next his hopes for an easier, more comfortable and bourgeois sainthood had gone up in smoke. The devil had undone all his plans. It now occurred to Luis that he could not even become a Christian Philemon, for slashing a fellow man's head with a saber blow was surely a poor beginning for a perpetual idyll.

After the agitation of that whole day, he was in the state of a man with brain fever.

Currito and the captain took him, each by an arm, and led him home between them.

* * *

When Don Pedro de Vargas was told that they were bringing his son home wounded, he sprang out of bed, greatly startled. He rushed to his side, examined the bruises and the wounded arm and saw there was no serious injury. But he cried out to heaven that he would avenge the offense and did not calm down until he had learned all about the duel, and how, in spite of his theology, Luis had proved able to avenge himself.

A little later the doctor came to treat Luis and predicted that he would be well enough to go out of the house in three or four days. But it would take months for the Count to recover. His life was not in danger, however. He had regained consciousness and had asked to be taken to his own village, not more than a league away from where these events had occurred. A carriage had been hired and had taken him home with his servants and the two strangers who had acted as his seconds.

Four days after these events, the doctor's prognosis was proved correct and Luis, still bruised from the blows, and with his wound not yet healed, was able to go out, and an early and complete recovery seemed assured.

As soon as he was on his feet, Luis thought the first duty before him was to confess to his father his love affair with Pepita and to declare his intention of marrying her.

During his son's illness Don Pedro had not visited his farms, for he had done nothing but look after his son, staying at his side, keeping him company, and spoiling him with marked affection.

On the morning of the 27th of June, after the doctor had left, Don Pedro was alone with his son. Whereupon the confession, so difficult for Luis came forth as follows: "Father," Luis said, "I must not go on deceiving you any longer. I'm going to confess my faults to you today and lay aside hypocrisy."

"Son, if what you want to do is make confession, it would be better to call the Vicar. My standards are very lax. I'll absolve you of anything, even though my absolution would be worthless. But if you want to confide some deep secret to me as to your best friend, go ahead. I'm listening."

"What I have to confess to you is a most grievous fault, and I'm ashamed of it . . ."

"Well, don't be ashamed before your father. Tell me all about it."

Then Luis said, blushing and visibly perturbed: "My secret is that I'm in love with . . . Pepita Jiménez, and she . . ."

Don Pedro interrupted his son with a shout of laughter and completed the sentence. ". . . And she's in love with you, and on Saint John's Eve you were sweet-talking her until two o'clock in the morning, and after that you picked a quarrel with the Count of Genazahar on account of her, and broke his head. Well, son, that's quite a secret you're telling me. There's not a dog or a cat in the village that doesn't already know all about everything. It looked as if the one thing that might possibly be concealed was the length of the meeting, until two o'clock in the morning, but some gypsy bun-sellers saw you leaving the house, and their tongues didn't stop wagging until they'd told every living soul. Pepita isn't concealing things any better either; and she's right, because it's no secret from anyone . . . Pepita has come here twice a day ever since you were hurt, and she's been sending Antoñona another two or three times to inquire about your health; and the only reason they haven't come in to see you is that I wouldn't let them because I didn't want them to upset you."

Luis's worry and dismay increased as he heard his father tell the whole story in laconic outline.

"What a surprise!" he said. "You must have been completely astonished."

"Neither surprised nor astonished, my boy. All those things have been known in the village for four days, and to tell the truth your transformation has become a nine-day wonder. 'Look how he hid his light under a bushel. Look how he got

his way. Look at the way sly-boots played possum!' That's what
people are saying now that everything has leaked out. The
Vicar has been especially dumfounded. He's still crossing himself to think how you labored in the vineyard of the Lord on
the night of the 23d and 24th, and how varied and diverse
your labors were. But except for your wound, the news gave
me no cause for alarm. We oldsters can hear the grass grow.
It's not so easy for a cockerel to fool a poultry dealer."

"It's true; I did try to deceive you. I've been a hypocrite."

"Don't be silly; I'm not trying to blame you. I'm making
myself out to be very wise. But let's be frank; I have no call to
boast. I've known the progress of your love affair with Pepita
step by step for more than two months now; but that's because
your uncle, the Dean, to whom you poured out your heart on
paper, has passed it all on to me. Listen to your uncle's accus-
ing letter, then listen to my answer, which is a very important
document of which I have kept a copy."

Don Pedro took some papers out of his pocket and read the
following:

The Dean's Letter:—"My dear brother. I'm truly sorry to
have to give you bad news, but I trust God will grant you the
patience and long-suffering not to be angry and bitter. Several
days ago Luisito began to write me some strange letters from
which I have discovered, beneath his mystical exaltation, a very
worldly and sinful attraction to a certain beautiful, young, mischievous, and very coquettish widow, who lives in your village.
Until now I had been deceiving myself, thinking Luisito's
vocation was very strong, and I flattered myself that I was giving to the Church of God a very wise, virtuous, and exemplary
priest in him. But the aforesaid letters have come to destroy
my illusions. Luisito shows himself in them as more of a poet
than a truly pious man, and the widow, who must be of the
ilk of Barrabas, will conquer him without lifting a finger. Al-

though I am writing to Luisito, admonishing him to flee from temptation, I feel certain that he will fall into it. I must not let this upset me, for if he is to fall short and become a gallant and a lover, it is better that his baser nature should show itself in time, and that he should not become a priest. So I can see no serious objection to Luisito's staying on there to be tried by the touchstone and weighed in the crucible of a love affair like that, with the little widow acting as the reagent that will either reveal the pure gold of his clerical virtues, or the dross with which the gold is mixed. But the stumbling block is that this widow, whom we are using as an assayer's scale, turns out to be the girl you're courting, and for all I know, in love with. It would be a devil of a mess if your son should become your rival. This would create a dreadful scandal, and in order to avoid that in time, I'm writing you now to send or bring Luisito back here on any pretext whatsoever, and the sooner the better."

Luis was listening in silence, with downcast eyes. His father went on, "I answered this letter from the Dean as follows:

Answer: "Dear brother and venerable spiritual father: Many thanks for the news you sent me and for your warnings and advice. Although I consider myself smart, I must confess my stupidity in this instance. I was blinded by vanity. From the time my son arrived, Pepita Jiménez showed herself so affable and affectionate toward me that I thought everything would be smooth sailing. Your letter was needed to open my eyes. I understand now that naughty Pepita was not thinking of me when she turned human, when she gave so many parties for me and danced attendance on me, except as the father of the beardless theologian. That awakening mortified and depressed me a little at first. That I can't deny. But then I thought it all over as befitted my years, and my mortification and depression turned to joy. The boy is good as gold. Since he's been with me, I've grown much fonder of him. I separated myself from him and turned him over to you to be educated because my life was not the most exemplary, and for that and other reasons, he would have grown up in this village like a savage. You surpassed my hopes and even my wishes by almost making a father of the Church out of Luisito. My vanity might have been flattered by having a saintly son, but I should have been sorry to be left without an heir to my house and name, who would give me fine grandchildren, and who would enjoy my wealth after my death, for I glory in my property because I have acquired it by working and planning, and without any cheating or sharp practice. Perhaps what made me decide to marry in order to secure my succession was that I was persuaded there was no other way; that Luis was slated to proselytize the Chinese, the Indians, and the pygmies of the Congo. Naturally, I fixed my eyes on Pepita Jiménez, a very pretty little girl, more blessed than heaven, and more loving than coquettish, not at all of the ilk of Barrabas, as you think. I hold such a high opinion of Pepita that if she were sixteen again, with an imperious mother who would force her against her will, and if I were eighty years old like Don Gumersindo, that is, if I were staring death in the face, I would take Pepita to wife so she would smile at me as I died, as though she were my guardian angel in human form, and so as to be able to leave her my position, my property, and my name. But Pepita is no longer sixteen; she's twenty. She is not under her crafty mother's thumb. Nor am I eighty; I'm fifty-five. I am at the worst age, for I'm beginning to feel the worse for wear, with a touch of asthma, a chronic cough, rheumatic twinges and other aches and pains, and yet I haven't the slightest desire to die. I think I shall live another twenty years, and as I am thirty-five years older than Pepita, think of the disastrous future that

would have awaited her with such a tough old man. For all her
goodness, she would have been bound to loathe me after a few
years of marriage. Just because she is good and discreet, she
never wished to accept me as a husband in spite of the insistence and stubbornness with which I've proposed to her.
How grateful I am for it now! Even my vanity, which was
wounded by her rejection, is soothed now by the thought that
if she doesn't love me, she does love my blood, for she has
chosen my son. If such a fresh and thriving shoot of ivy does
not want to cling to the old tree, a little worm-eaten now, it can
climb up, I tell myself, to the top of the green and flourishing
sapling. God bless them both and prosper their love. Far from
sending the boy back to you, I shall keep him here, by force if
necessary. I am prepared to plot against his vocation. I'm dreaming now of seeing him married. It will rejuvenate me to watch
that young couple united in love. Not to mention when the
little ones start coming. Won't it be better for Luisito to do
his preaching at home and give me an abundance, a series, of
little rosy blonde catechumens with eyes like Pepita's, looking
like cherubim without wings, instead of going out as a missionary and bringing home several neophytes from Australia, or
Madagascar, or India, with lips an inch thick, black as ink, or
yellow as leather, and owl-eyed? I'd have to hold any catechumens he might bring me from abroad at arm's length, for fear
they'd taint me, whereas the home-made kind would smell to
me of the roses of paradise and would kiss me and call me
grandfather, and pat me on the bald spot I'm acquiring. What
more can I ask? When I was in my prime I never thought of
domestic delights, but now that I'm nearing old age, if not already there, I rejoice in the hope of playing the role of
patriarch, as I am not likely to become a cenobite. And don't
think I'm going to limit myself to merely hoping that the new
couple will suit each other. I'm going to work hard to help

them adjust. If Pepita is to be the crucible and Luis the metal, in keeping with your analogy, I shall seek or have already found a most serviceable bellows or forge that will help to keep the fire blazing so that the metal may soon liquefy. This bellows is Antonoña, Pepita's nurse, a very artful, close-mouthed woman, and very fond of her mistress. Antonoña and I understand each other, and through her I know that Pepita is all aswoon with love. We've agreed that I shall go on conniving and making out that I don't know a thing. The Vicar, one of God's own, is as useful to me as Antonoña, or more so, without knowing it, for he keeps talking forever to Pepita about Luis, and to Luis about Pepita. The result is that this excellent man, with half a century on each foot, has been transformed—oh, miracle of love and innocence!—into a carrier pigeon through whom the lovers send each other messages and compliments, both also quite unaware. Such a potent combination of natural and artificial means must infallibly bear fruit. I shall let you know before I announce the wedding, so that you can come and perform the ceremony, or else send the sweethearts your blessing and a nice present."

When Don Pedro had finished reading his letter, and turned to look at Luis, he saw that Luis had been listening with his eyes swimming in tears.

The father and son clasped each other in a long and close embrace.

* * *

Exactly a month after this conversation and this reading, the marriage of Luis de Vargas and Pepita Jiménez took place.

The Dean excused himself on the grounds of his work and declined to come, though he sent his blessing and a gift of a pair of beautiful earrings for Pepita. He was afraid that his brother would poke too much fun at him because Luisito's mysticism had come to naught, and he knew, also, that his stay in the village would be somewhat awkward, because everyone would be saying that he was a poor hand at making saints.

Consequently, the Vicar had the pleasure of marrying Pepita to Luis.

The bride, very elegantly dressed, looked beautiful and well worth the hair shirt and scourges whose place she was taking.

Don Pedro gave a stupendous ball that evening in the patio of his house and the adjoining parlors. Servants and masters, nobles and day-laborers, ladies and young ladies, and the village girls all attended and mingled as in the legendary first age of the world, called golden, though I don't know why. Four skilled, or if not skilled, tireless guitarists played the fandango. Two famous singers, a gypsy man and woman, sang highly amorous verses, appropriate to the circumstances. And the schoolmaster read an epithalamium in heroic verse.

The commoners feasted on fried puff paste, fritters, honey cakes, crullers, almond cakes, frosted cakes and an abundance of wine.

The gentry were regaled with preserves, chocolate, orange-blossom honey, and sugar-cane syrup, plus various kinds of sweet spiced drinks and fragrant and delicate punches.

Don Pedro was like a young recruit again—boisterous, full of jokes, and gallant. What he had told the Dean about his rheumatism and other chronic ailments seemed a lie. He danced the fandango with Pepita, with his prettiest servants, and with half a dozen other girls. As he returned each of his exhausted partners to her chair, he would give her the prescribed embrace with proper effusiveness, and he pinched the less serious girls, even though this forms no part of the ritual. Indeed he carried his gallantry to the extreme of leading Doña

Casilda onto the dance floor. She could not refuse, and what with her two hundred and more pounds of humanity and the July heat, she was shedding rivers of sweat from every pore. Finally, Don Pedro stuffed Currito so full of food and made him drink so many toasts to the happiness of the newlyweds, that Dientes, the muleteer, had to take him home to sleep it off, slung across a donkey's back like a wineskin.

The dance lasted until three o'clock in the morning, but the newlyweds discreetly slipped away before eleven and went to Pepita's house. Once more Luis entered that clean bedroom, which barely a month earlier he had entered in the dark, full of anxiety and confusion, this time by lamp light, with pomp and majesty, and like an adored lord and master.

Although it was the invariable use and custom of the village to give every widower or widow who remarried a terrific charivari, thus shattering their peace with the noise of the bells and horns during the first night of their nuptials, Pepita was so well-liked, Don Pedro so respected, and Luis so beloved, that the charivari was omitted that night, and no attempt at one was made. That in itself was an event so rare that it is recalled in the village chronicles.

III

EPILOGUE

The story of Pepita and Luisito really should end here. This epilogue is superfluous, but the Dean had it in his file, and although we shall not publish it in its entirety, we shall do so in part and give at least a sample.

No one should entertain the least doubt that Luis and Pepita lived for many long years, enjoying all the happiness and peace that earth can hold, united in an overwhelming love, more or less the same age, she beautiful, he handsome and charming, both discreet and full of good works. But this, a well-drawn dialectic conclusion to most people, becomes a certainty to whoever reads the Epilogue.

The Epilogue also gives some news of the secondary characters who appear in the narrative, and whose fate might perhaps be of interest to readers.

The Epilogue boils down to a collection of letters sent to his brother the Dean by Don Pedro de Vargas, dating from the wedding and continuing for four years.

We shall pass on here some few and brief fragments from the said letters in chronological order, but omitting dates, and then write finis to the story.

Luis shows the keenest gratitude to Antonoña, without whose good offices he would not have married Pepita. But this woman who was an accomplice to the one mistake that he and Pepita had made, so much an intimate of the household and so well-informed about everything, could hardly fail to be a disturbing element. To be free of her and yet do her a service, Luis has arranged for her to go back to her husband, whose daily drunkenness she had not cared to put up with. This man, the son of Cencias, the teacher, has promised that he will *almost* never get drunk again, but he did not go so far as to promise a ringing "never." Antonoña put her faith in this half-promise, however, and consented to go back beneath the conjugal roof-tree. After the couple had been reunited, Luis considered the homeopathic method might be conducive to effectively curing Cencias's son. He had heard that those who work in pastry shops come to hate sweets, and inferred from that that tavern-keepers should develop an abhorrence of wine and brandy. Accordingly, he sent Antonoña and her husband to the capital of this province where he set them up in a magnificent tavern at his own expense. They're living there contentedly; they've saved a good deal of money, and probably they'll end up by being rich. He still gets drunk at times; but Antonoña, a very strong woman, usually gives him such a good drubbing for it that he may eventually reform.

Observing and envying the domestic happiness of Pepita and Luis, Currito wanted to imitate his cousin, for whom his admiration mounts every day, and he therefore hastily sought a sweetheart and married the daughter of a rich local farmer. The girl is healthy, good-looking, rosy as a poppy, and she promises to acquire shortly a greater volume and density than her mother-in-law, Doña Casilda.

The Count of Genazahar has now recovered from his injury, after five months in bed, and has mended his insolent ways, they say. Not long ago he paid Pepita more than half of his debt, and has requested an extension of time to repay the remainder.

We have sustained a great loss, although it had long been foreseen. The Vicar, yielding to the weight of his years, has gone on to a better life. Pepita was at his bedside to the end, and she closed his half-opened mouth with her beautiful hands. The Vicar died like a blessed servant of God. More than death, it seemed the felicitous passage to happier regions. Nevertheless, Pepita and all the rest of us have sincerely mourned him. He left only five or six dollars and his furniture, for he had given away everything. The poor here would have been orphaned by his death if it were not for Pepita.

Everyone in the village is mourning the death of the Vicar, and some consider him a real saint, worthy of being placed on the altars. Miracles are being attributed to him. I don't know about that; but I do know that he was a fine man who must have gone straight to heaven, where we shall have an intercessor in him. Yet his humility, his modesty and his God-fearing qualities were such that at the hour of his death he spoke of his sins as if he actually had some, and asked us to pray to the Lord and to Mary Most Holy that he might be forgiven them.

This exemplary life and death of a man, simple and dull-witted though he was, but of good will, of deep faith, and of fervent charity, have made a deep impression on Luis's mind. He compares himself with the Vicar, and says he feels humbled. This has weighted his heart with a kind of bitter melancholy, but Pepita wisely dissipates it with smiles and affection.

Everything is prospering here at home. Luis and I have wine-cellars that cannot be beaten in Spain, if we except Jerez. The olive harvest has been superb this year. We can indulge ourselves in all manner of luxuries, and I am advising Luis and Pepita to take a trip to Germany, France, and Italy so that Pepita can get away from her cares and restore herself. Without being extravagant or improvident, the children could spend several thousand dollars on the trip, and bring back fine books, good furniture, and *objets d'art* to decorate their house.

We have delayed the christening two weeks so that it could fall on the same day as the first anniversary of their wedding. The child is as beautiful as the sun and very robust. I am the godfather and we gave him my name. I'm dreaming now of the day when Periquito can talk and say amusing things.

It now turns out, according to letters from Havana, that to make everything come out right for these married lovers, Pepita's brother, whose rascality we considered a disgrace to the family, is now about to do it honor by becoming something like a personage. During the long period when we knew nothing about him, he was making good use of his opportunities and luck began to smile on him. He got a new position in the Customs Service; he did some trading in slaves, then he went bankrupt, which for certain businessmen is like a good pruning for a tree, making them grow all the better. Today he is so prosperous that he is determined to enter the ranks of the aristocracy, with the title of Marquess or Duke.

Pepita is worried and somewhat scandalized at this turn of fortune, but I tell her not to be foolish. Her brother is and always will be a rascal, so isn't it better for him to be a rascal under a lucky star?

We could go on giving extracts, were it not for the fear of wearying our readers. Let us conclude, then, by copying a portion of one of the last letters.

My children have come back from their trip in good health, with Periquito very mischievous and beautiful.

Luis and Pepita have made up their minds not to leave the village again, even if they should live longer than Philemon and Bauchus. They are more in love than ever.

They brought back some beautiful furniture, many books, some paintings, and I don't know how many elegant knick-nacks, which they bought abroad, principally in Paris, Rome, Florence, and Vienna.

The elegance and good taste with which they have furnished their house will do much to implant and spread the amenities of culture, just as the affection they have for each other and the tenderness and cordiality of their treatment of each other and everyone else has exercised a good influence on local manners.

The people in Madrid are given to saying that we villagers are geese and oafs, but they stay where they are and never take the trouble to come here and polish us. On the other hand, nearly ever village dweller who is knowledgeable and worthwhile, or thinks he is, is not satisfied until he has cleared out, leaving the country and the villages of the provinces abandoned.

Pepita and Luis are following the opposite course, and I applaud them with all my heart.

They are improving and beautifying everything to make this nook their Eden.

You must not think, however, that Luis's and Pepita's fondness for material goods has cooled their religious feeling in the least. Their piety grows deeper each day, and in each pleasure or satisfaction they enjoy or can share with their neighbors, they see a new blessing from Heaven, for which they feel more deeply obligated to show their gratitude. They know that that satisfaction and that contentment would not be theirs, would lack price, value, and substance, if the awareness and the firm belief in divine grace did not lend it to them.

Amidst his present good fortune, Luis has never forgotten the collapse of the ideal he had dreamed of. There are moments when his present life seems to him vulgar, selfish, and prosaic compared with the life of sacrifice, the spiritual life he believed himself called to in the early years of his youth. But Pepita hastens solicitously to dispel such melancholy thoughts, and Luis then realizes and maintains that man may serve God in any state or walk of life, and he strikes a balance between this lawful love for the earthly and the transient and lively faith and love of God which fill his soul. But he places a kind of divine base under it all, for without that the stars which populate the firmament, the flowers and fruits that beautify the fields, Pepita's eyes, and the innocence and beauty of Periquito would seem to him unworthy of love. Without his provident God, he says, the wide world, all that grand fabric of the universe would still seem sublime, but lacking in order, beauty, or plan. As for the lesser world, the term by which he designates man, he would not love it either, if it were not for God. He loves mankind not because God has commanded him to do so, but because the dignity of man and his deserving to be loved rest on God Himself, who not only created the human soul in His image, but also ennobled the human body, making of it a living temple to the Holy Ghost in communion with Him through the Sacrament, thus elevating man to union with the Word made Flesh. For these and other reasons, which I cannot explain here, Luis consoles himself and accepts the fact that he was not meant to be a mystical, ecstatic, and apostolic man, and casts aside the kind of generous envy he felt toward the Vicar on the day of his death. But both he and Pepita continue with great Christian devotion to give thanks to God for the good they enjoy, finding no basis, reason, or cause for this goodness but God Himself.

There are some rooms in my children's house that look like beautiful little Catholic chapels or oratories. But I must confess that both of them also have a touch of paganism, like pastoral love-poetry that has gone to find shelter outside its own boundaries.

Pepita's garden is no longer a garden; it has become a beautifully landscaped tract planted to pines, Indian fig-trees, which grow here in the open air, and a well-arranged hothouse, small but filled with rare plants.

The pavilion or summer house where we ate strawberries that afternoon, the second time that Pepita and Luis met and spoke to each other, has been transformed into an airy gazebo with a portico and columns of white marble. Inside it is a spacious room with comfortable furniture. Two beautiful paintings adorn it: one shows Psyche discovering Cupid by lamplight and gazing at him in ecstasy as he sleeps on their bed; another shows Chloe with the fleeing cicada in her bosom where in such pleasant shade it thinks itself safe and begins to sing as Daphnis tries to remove it.

A skillful copy of the Medici Venus in Carrara marble occupies the choicest spot and presides over the room, as it were. On the plinth there is an engraving in letters of gold of the following verses by Lucretius:

Nec sine te quidquam dias in luminis oras
Exoritur, neque fit laetum, neque amabile quidquam.[56]

* * *

---

[56] *Nor does aught rise into the aura of divine light without thee, nor anything joyous or lovely come to be.*

Lucretius, De rerum naturae